W9-AGU-666

Princess Shayna's Invisible Visible Gift

#76

DEAR MEKSHAN~
I HOPE YOU WILL
ENJOY YOUR JOURNEY
WITH PRINCESS SHAYNA.
THANKS FOR ALL YOUR
CREATIVE SUPPORT!
Sheila Glazov
2/25/97

Written by Sheila Glazov
and illustrated by Len Birnbaum

© 1997 by Sheila Glazov

Published by:
    Peridot Productions
    24714 Nodding Flower Court
    Tower Lakes, IL 60010
    Phone: (847) 526-9039
    Fax: (847) 526-4187

All rights reserved. No part of this book may be reproduced or transmitted in any form or by any means, electronic or mechanical, including photocopying, recording or by any information storage and retrieval system, without written permission from the author.

Library of Congress Catalog Card Number: 96-92963

Printed in the United States of America

Publisher's **Cataloging-in-Publication Data**

Glazov, Sheila N.
Princess shayna's invisible visible gift/Sheila N. Glazov
        p.   cm.

Summary: *Princess Shayna's Invisible Visible Gift* is a fairy tale to teach children and adults how to enhance and strengthen their self-esteem, understand and respect themselves and others who are different than they are, develop their creative problem solving skills and build positive and nurturing communities within their homes, schools, businesses, and neighborhoods. A portion of the book's profit will be donated to diabetes research and education.

1. Self-esteem—Fiction. 2. Fairy tales. 3. Parent and child—Fiction.
4. Diabetes—Fiction. 5. Creative thinking—Fiction. 6. Family—Fiction.
I. Title

[Fic] - dc21

ISBN: 0-9655619-9-2 $18.95 softcover

Dedication

My book is dedicated to the following individuals, who are as valuable and exceptional to me as Princess Shayna's village emissaries and the sapphire gemstones for which they are named. Each person has contributed to the positive, loving, and supportive community that inspired and encouraged me to write my "community parable," *Princess Shayna's Invisible Visible Gift*.

My parents, "King" Alexander and "Queen" Sylvia for giving me the Invisible Visible Gift.

My husband, Jordan, who is the beloved and devoted "White Falcon" in my life.

My children, Joshua, Noah, Alex, and Peter, and my grandchildren, Matthew and Samantha, who are the "silver apricots" in my life.

Pappa Joe "Lord Joseph," Grandma Lil "Lady Lillian," Mimi "Lady Eva," Poppy "Lord Harry," Aunt Sarah "Sarah Spundah," Uncle Sig "Sigmund the Wizard," Miss Cohen "Mac," and Mort, who are the gingko tree roots and foundation of my life.

My dear friends, Michelle "Lady Michelle" and John "Lord John," Lenny and Margie, my brother, Mark "Lord Markus" and sister-in-law, Janet "Jani, Queen of the Flower Fairies," whose love, friendship and talents are the strong trunk of the gingko tree that I have leaned on for support.

All my friends and colleagues who have been my gingko tree leaflets and the community that has helped me grow by sharing their gifts of knowledge, balance, and guidance.

My talented friend, Lenny, for sharing his magnificent artistic gift with all of us.

My devoted friend, Michelle, for sharing her incredible teaching gift with all of us.

My knowledgeable friend, Jody, for sharing her "colors" gift.

My encouraging friend, Mari Pat, for sharing her gift of storytelling.

My skillful friends, Janet, Theresa, and Barbara for sharing their book production gifts.

My "author-artist" friend, Carol, for offering her peaceful wisdom gift.

My creative friend, Carol, for sharing her gift of CPSI.

Last, but not least, my generous friend, Reg, for sharing his thank you gift: "Great gift to the group. Thanks, Reg."*

*It was Reg's little "orange" note at CPSI in June 1995 that was my "Rimsiyavyo!" to write *Princess Shayna's Invisible Visible Gift*.

To all of you, my heartfelt "Village of the Blue Forget-Me-Nots" appreciation for sharing your most praiseworthy gifts with me. I love you more than tongue can tell!

Gift Givers

Sheila Glazov, Author

Sheila Glazov, SP, is the managing member of VISIONEER®, LLC and a professional speaker. She has more than 25 years experience in education and business. Sheila has taught third and fourth grades and English as a second language. She is an adjunct faculty member at William Rainey Harper College, a True Colors® certified trainer, and a guest instructor at Northwood University, Alden B. Dow Creativity Center, and DePaul University, Kellstadt Graduate School of Management.

Sheila earned a BS degree in education from Ohio State University, a degree in creative leadership from Disney University, and is a graduate of the Creative Problem Solving Institute General Facilitation Program and of the McNellis Creative Planning Institute.

Who's Who in American Women listed Sheila in its 1997, 20th anniversary issue, and in 1995 *Today's Chicago Woman* newspaper recognized her as one of "100 Women Making a Difference" for her entrepreneurial achievements in the field of creativity. Sheila also is an active member in several professional and community associations and was cofounder of the Eastern Sierra Jewish Community Synagogue.

Sheila and her husband, Jordan, have been married for 30 years and have been business partners since 1982. They also have raised three children and delight in their two grandchildren.

If you are interested in contacting Sheila regarding her customized interactive presentations about self-esteem, creativity, team building, communications, leadership, and personal and professional development, you may call her at (847) 526-9039.

If you would like to order additional copies of *Princess Shayna's Invisible Visible Gift* contact: Armstrong Distribution at (888) 382-2767.

Len Birnbaum, Illustrator

Len is a graduate of the School of the Chicago Art Institute and the Chicago Academy of Fine Arts. Len has been recognized for his artistic talents for more than 50 years. He received the Artist Guild of Chicago "Gold Brush" Award, the U.S. Holocaust Memorial Museum citation, the Rabbi Philip L. Lipis "Lamed" Award, and numerous first place and best-of-show ribbons in many Chicagoland art shows. Len has also illustrated two other books, consulted on several architectural projects, and worked with Norman Rockwell, Ludwig Wolpert, and Mal Ahlgren.

In 1992 Len became semi-retired after many successful careers in the world of commercial art and advertising. Now he devotes himself to illustrating, consulting, and enjoying more time with his wife Marge. Married for 50 years, Len and Marge have raised four children and delight in their five grandchildren. Sheila and "Lenny" and their families have enjoyed the gift of friendship for more than 26 years.

Michelle Bracken, Educational Consultant

Michelle earned a BS degree in speech and hearing pathology at Ohio State University, a master of arts degree in speech and hearing pathology from Cleveland State University, and a permanent certification in special education from Hofstra University. Michelle has been a special education teacher for 16 years. She also was a speech and hearing therapist for Cleveland public schools and the New York United Cerebral Palsy Association and taught English in Israel.

Michelle also is an instructor in the New York State United Teachers Effective Teaching Program and teaches lifelong learning skills programs to other teachers to enhance their effectiveness in the classroom.

Michelle and her husband John have been married for 20 years and raised three children, delight in their five grandchildren and are Sheila and Jordan's children's Godparents. Sheila and "Shelley" were roommates in college and have shared the "treasured gifts of true friendship" and the blessings of their family for 33 years.

Table of Contents

Princess Shayna's Invisible Visible Gift and the *Gift Giver's Guide* is meant to be read and enjoyed by both children and adults. It is designed to encourage people to enjoy alone or read to one another. I believe it is essential for youngsters and adults to read aloud to one another, to develop their listening skill and keep their creativity alive. It is vital that people understand that sharing their ideas about the story with each other will become an important tool for opening the channels for skillful communications and building their self-esteem. I hope the individual chapters will also be used as a resource guide for developing creative problem solving skills.

The *Gift Giver's Guide* at the end of the book will assist the reader and listener to reflect upon what was meaningful in the chapters they read and help them to create the opportunities for personal interpretation and cooperative interaction. It can be used after reading each chapter or at the conclusion of the story.—Sheila Glazov

"A stunning allegory with particular emphasis on the importance of accepting others and positive self-esteem. Once the reader picks up this book . . . and starts enjoying its message and its meaning, he or she will not put it down."

Arnold "Nick" Carter
Vice President Communications Research, Nightingale-Conant Corporation

"This charming fairy tale provides an imaginative and entertaining way of teaching about diversity and individualism; a great teaching tool for students of *all* ages!"

Carol Coppage
Executive director, Alden B. Dow Creativity Center, Northwood University

"A remarkably beautiful parable about the importance of a loving foundation so risks and obstacles are overcome not by searching for safety in isolation, but through embracing the wisdom and miracles of a larger community."

Anne Hamilton Martin, PhD, Psychotherapist

"A fairy tale that speaks in many layers. A story for any family facing a challenging situation, and through love, understanding, respect, and some sacrifice there is a successful outcome."

Libby Gant-Davis, RD, CDE
Registered Dietitian and Certified Diabetes Educator

"The book comes at a time when most Americans are recognizing the importance of values and community in development of individuals' self-esteem. The eloquent metaphoric messages provide a valuable guide for adults and professionals searching for a message that brings meaning and connectedness in a difficult time."

Ellen A. Sherman, PhD, LMFT

"My brother and I like reading your book very much. We enjoy reading about Princess Shayna and Meevillain's evil plans. My favorite character is Princess Shayna and my brother's is Sigi. We really hope you write more books."

Carolyn, age 8, and Craig, age 5

"The *Gift Giver's Guide* gave me the opportunity to talk with my child about taking responsibility for our health. By asking him questions, we were able to share many wonderful and special bedtimes."

Joanna Slan, Author
I'm Too Blessed To Be Depressed

"Sheila's rare vision, awareness, and respect for her princess and her readers reflect her talent as both an 'author-artist' and a 'self-esteem artist' in one delightful, original, and important book that honors and celebrates us all!"

Carol Owens Campbell, Author
Views from a Pier: Visions of Hope - - - - Dreams - - - - Awareness - - - - and Peace

"Sheila Glazov's creativity brings vibrant color to a sometimes gray world and challenges the rest of us to find that special shade that is truly ourselves."

Kevin E. O'Connor, CSP, Author
When All Else Fails: Finding Solutions to Your Most Persistent Management Problems

"It's a 'love gift' from Sheila Glazov to all of us. Guaranteed to make us feel safe through our own quest for self-discovery."

Jody Lewis,
President, Jody Lewis and Associates, StHr Quality Service

"Princess Shayna allowed me to make *her* story *my* story."

Mari Pat Varga
The Creative Communications Coach, Mari Pat Varga and Associates

Foreword

I am Peridot, the emissary from the Village of the Green Healing Herbs. As you will read in *Princess Shayna's Invisible Visible Gift*, I am the official chronicler of Princess Shayna's Vision Quest. I am very honored to write this foreword to Sheila Glazov's community parable.

Sheila believes people develop positive self-esteem when there is a supportive community to nurture them. Her vision and goal is to teach adults and children to understand and respect themselves as well as others who are different than they are. When they do, they can enhance and strengthen their self-esteem and build that strong and nurturing community within their homes, schools, neighborhoods, businesses, and organizations. Then they can share their most praiseworthy gifts, just as the villagers do in this story.

The title, *Princess Shayna's Invisible Visible Gift,* comes from Sheila's premise: self-esteem is invisible when you give it to someone, and visible upon them when they receive it, but only if they are willing to share their gift with others. The Yiddish word *shayna* means beautiful, and self-esteem is a beautiful gift!

The gingko tree on the cover represents the story's three main themes of building self-esteem:

1. The tree's roots represent the foundation and the "village elders" from which we grow physically, emotionally, and spiritually.

2. The tree trunk represents our parents, family members, friends, teachers, and mentors who we all lean on for support, depending on the circumstances.

3. The leaves grow in leaflet clusters, like a community. The branches of leaf clusters grow upward and represent the youth in all of us, reaching for new knowledge with balance and guidance from the roots and solid support from the trunk.

The oldest species of tree, the gingko is more than 125 million years old. The Chinese culture considers the gingko to be a tree of great distinction and dignity. It also is an ancient Chinese emblem of longevity and survival, and it is respected as a loyal and historic soul, as are the village elders in the story.

The gingko tree is historically known as the grandfather-grandson tree. Only the old trees bear seeds, so it is the grandson of the planter who benefits from the precious "silver apricots" of the tree. This is very meaningful because the roots of the story were planted by Sheila's father, who had Type II diabetes and was the inspiration for King Alexander in her story; and her elder son, Joshua, who was diagnosed with Type I diabetes when he was 15, will benefit from the fruits of his mother's story. A portion of this book's profit will be donated to diabetes research and education.

What distinguishes a fairy tale from other stories is the fact that it speaks to the very heart and soul of the child within all of us. I believe that everyone can relate to this fairy tale. Princess Shayna's story confirms that life can present difficulties, but with good self-esteem and a loving, supportive environment (home, school, work, neighborhood, community, etc.), we all can develop the courage to meet life's obstacles and turn them into opportunities, just as Princess Shayna does.

The story also acknowledges the significant fact that no one is perfect, not even a princess. This message is important not only to people who have diabetes, but to others who face different challenges in their lives.

As an educator and businesswoman, Sheila strongly believes that positive self-esteem helps people become good decision makers and creative problem solvers. Think about the decisions you have made when you were feeling good about yourself and the decisions you made when you were not.

I invite you to discover the many thought-provoking and enchanting messages within this fairy tale. The author and I hope you will enjoy yourself as you share *Princess Shayna's Invisible Visible Gift*, her Vision Quest, and your own journey of self-discovery!

Peridot

Emissary from the Village of the Green Healing Herbs

Kingdom of Kindness

*L*ong, long ago in a distant land, there lived a trustworthy and generous king named Alexander. Winding through his Kingdom of Kindness was a beautiful sparkling river, which fed four serenely flowing streams that connected the four villages of the kingdom. The streams flowed each into the other as they circled King Alexander's spired castle atop a gently rolling hill. Surrounding the castle was the Forest of Friendship, a tranquil forest that spread as far as the eye could see.

King Alexander had built a royal arboretum for all the people in the Kingdom of Kindness to enjoy. This magnificent garden, which he called The Garden of Knowledge, was located inside the castle grounds and was encircled by an ivy-covered wall. This wall was not a barrier, but a sign of friendship and an ever-growing framework for many varieties of trees, flowers, and healing herbs that the king cultivated. King Alexander gained much joy from planting and nurturing the flowers and herbs in his garden.

During King Alexander's 34th gala birthday celebration, the king confided in his most trusted confidant and faithful friend, Sigmund the Royal Wizard.

1

King Alexander said, "There are many learned and interesting people in the Kingdom of Kindness and from many distant lands with whom I study and enjoy the activities of my royal court. You know I have chosen to wait for many years to marry, but lately I have been very melancholy. I miss sharing my life with a wife and family. I will search for a special woman to be my queen and to make my life complete. But, she must have a great spirit of love and sense of tradition."

After his birthday celebration, King Alexander summoned his four royal advisors to his royal library and said, "I have decided to search for a queen to return happiness to my life and the entire Kingdom of Kindness. I decree that on my 35th birthday I will marry. A year of planning and preparation for my marriage shall begin today. Throughout the year, I will host grand festivities with the hope of meeting my future queen.

It was a very busy year filled with many grand festivities in the royal castle. The brightest and most beautiful young women from the Kingdom of Kindness and many distant lands were in attendance. But to everyone's dismay and disappointment, not one of the young women touched King Alexander's heart and soul.

Then, one month before King Alexander's 35th birthday, he was walking through his Garden of Knowledge. He noticed an unusually beautiful and elegant young woman reading under the lacy canopy of his favorite honey locust tree, surrounded by a blanket of delicate lilies of the valley. The morning sunlight that filtered through the honey locust tree illuminated the young woman's fairy-kissed freckles on her delicate skin. Her magnificent cascading copper-colored hair bedazzled the king.

The young woman looked to be much younger than the king, but when she spoke he recognized a wisdom well beyond her years. King Alexander immediately knew she was the woman he had been waiting for.

Recognizing the king, the young woman said, "I am Lady Sylvia, from the Village of the Yellow Sunflowers, where we value the spirit of family love and tradition." As Lady Sylvia gently spoke, the king could see that she had been raised with a great spirit of independence and a strong sense of thoughtfulness and caring.

For three joyful weeks, King Alexander and Lady Sylvia met in the Garden of Knowledge. When they announced their betrothal, there was jubilation throughout the kingdom.

One week later, just as he had promised, King Alexander and Lady Sylvia were married on his 35th birthday. Their wedding took place in the Garden of Knowledge under the honey locust tree surrounded by the lilies of the valley, where the king and his bride had first met.

The many wedding guests brought extraordinary gifts and treasures to celebrate the royal union. Even Princess Meevillain, who was enraged when the king had not chosen her as his bride, gave King Alexander and Queen Sylvia an unusual gift—a gold, jewel-encrusted decanter of nuptial nectar. Attached to the decanter were special instructions that only the king and queen could drink the nuptial nectar. They read:

"Enjoy this wedding gift with love only for one another,
For complete and loving devotion, throughout your life together.
Sealed with your wedding kiss, for your eternal wedded bliss,
A gift for only the two of you, replenished forever and ever!"

In the years to come, the Garden of Knowledge and the Kingdom of Kindness blossomed and flourished, as did the king and queen's love for one another. Yes, happiness had returned to King Alexander and his Kingdom of Kindness.

Visitors came from distant lands to experience the cooperative spirit within the kingdom. Each village was unique. The villagers developed their own expertise, and they shared their knowledge and skills with one another. They also respected each other's different styles of work and family life. The kingdom prospered because the people felt good about themselves and their accomplishments.

King Alexander and Queen Sylvia were completely devoted to one another and blissfully married. Yet they were without the joyful blessing of a child.

One morning, as the king and queen strolled through their garden, Queen Sylvia shared her deep sadness with her beloved husband. "I am so disappointed by the absence of a child in our life."

The king comforted the queen. "I, too, feel your disappointment. I will seek the advice of

3

Sigmund the Royal Wizard," King Alexander said gently.

The king went directly to Sigmund's chamber in the royal castle. "Good morning," Sigmund said to King Alexander.

"Not for Queen Sylvia and me," the king replied.

"What troubles my beloved king and queen?" Sigmund questioned.

"Queen Sylvia and I are deeply saddened because we do not have the joyful blessing of a child," King Alexander replied.

Sigmund listened and then replied, "I, too, feel your sadness, and I will do everything within my powers to help you. I will never forget how your grandfather warmly welcomed me into your family when I had to flee my homeland. I was thankful that my ancient Cush traditions, knowledge and skills were accepted in your kingdom. I was respected and immediately felt good about myself. Happiness had returned to my life."

Sigmund embraced his beloved king and said, "I will return to my chambers to create a solution to your problem. I give you my word."

For many months, Sigmund tried everything within his powers to create a solution for the royal couple's dilemma. He became so discouraged by his unsuccessful efforts that he finally went to the royal dining chamber to tell the king he could not keep his word. He had failed to create a solution for the king and queen's problem. As he approached the royal dining table, Sigmund noticed that the king had just poured a glass of nuptial nectar from Meevillain's wedding gift for himself and Queen Sylvia, but the King did not offer any to Sigmund.

"Rimsiyavyo!" Sigmund exclaimed in his ancient Cush language. Gently tapping the decanter of nuptial nectar with his cane, he said, "This is the cause of your dilemma!"

Sigmund explained his theory to the King and Queen. "When Meevillain's powerful magic was not strong enough to cause the King to fall in love with her, she was deeply angered. To appease her fury, she created a secret wedding spell of revenge—this powerful nuptial nectar. After your wedding celebration, she fled back to her mysterious kingdom to a life of solitude, sorrow, and sorcery!"

"Sigmund, what a brilliant theory," King Alexander and Queen Sylvia said.

Sigmund took leave of the king and queen and quickly returned to his royal chamber, where he began to contemplate a plan to create an antidote for Meevillain's nuptial nectar.

Later that night, Sigmund returned to the royal library and told the king and queen, "I shall journey to wherever Meevillain can be found. I know that my age might hinder me, but your trust and love will be my strength."

"Sigmund, we are concerned for your well-being. Such a journey could put your life at risk. We do not wish you to go, but we know we cannot keep you from your mission," the king and queen replied.

Sigmund said, "I am sure that I can secure the secret of Meevillain's powerful nuptial nectar and persuade her to tell me the ingredients to make an antidote. Then, and only then, will I be able to create a solution to your problem and help to bring you the joyful blessing of a child.

*You will find reflections about this chapter
on page 104 of the* Gift Giver's Guide.

Magic Potions

At daybreak, Sigmund decided to take a peaceful walk in the Forest of Friendship that encircled the royal castle. There he could contemplate how he would find Meevillain. He strolled through the forest, enjoying the silent beauty and peacefulness of his surroundings. He did not realize how long he had been walking and how tired he had become.

Sigmund was following a path along one of the four serenely flowing streams when he became very tired. "I am so exhausted from worry and fear of what will happen if I cannot find Meevillain. This large moss-covered rock that is blocking my path is a perfect place to rest for a while," he said to himself.

Before long Sigmund drifted off into a deep slumber. Suddenly, he was wakened by a chilling wind. He opened his eyes to see a frightfully mysterious woman dressed in raven-colored velvet from head to toe. She held a triple-twisted staff made from branches of the creeping willow, cyprus, and elder trees. She moved closer to Sigmund into the shadow of the large rock. Slowly, she removed the hood that shielded her face from sunlight.

Sigmund was startled by Meevillain's chilling presence. "Welcome to my Forest of Fear," Meevillain said.

Sigmund was astonished to see how Princess Meevillain had changed. He remembered what an enchanting young woman she was when she attended the royal wedding. How frightfully strange she looked now. Her beguiling smile had become a tortured frown.

"I am surprised to see you in the Forest of Friendship, Meevillain," Sigmund said as he slowly arose from his peaceful resting place.

The longer Meevillain spoke to Sigmund, the more she revealed her sense of self-importance. She began to think that Sigmund's interest in her had a deeper meaning. "Have you come to bring me news that King Alexander now desires *me* as his queen?" Meevillain questioned.

"No, I seek you out for another purpose," Sigmund replied.

Meevillain wanted to fly into a violent rage, but she contained herself because she was very interested in what Sigmund had to say.

Sigmund continued, "I journeyed into the Forest of Friendship to contemplate how to begin my royal quest. I must find the greatest magician in the entire world, one who can help me find a cure for King Alexander's and Queen Sylvia's dilemma and despair of childlessness."

"I am the greatest magician in all the world, and I can prove it to you, but only if you agree that I will become the royal wizard upon your death," Meevillain boasted confidently.

With a wild whirling motion of her staff, Meevillain showed Sigmund how she could kill all the graceful trees and delicate flowers in the forest and immediately bring them back to life on her command. Meevillain laughed and said, "At any moment, I can change any part of the Forest of Friendship into my Forest of Fear!"

"That was quite good, but not good enough to become the king's royal wizard," Sigmund told Meevillain. "Only a cure for King Alexander's and Queen Sylvia's dilemma and despair will be proof!" Sigmund demanded.

Meevillain hautily responded, "I'll have you know that it was *my* secret magic, a wedding spell of revenge, *my* very powerful nuptial nectar in *my* extraordinary gold, jewel-encrusted decanter that always replenishes itself that made your beloved King Alexander and Queen Sylvia childless!"

Sigmund pretended that he was astonished. "I will need proof of your powerful secret magic spell," he told Meevillain.

Meevillain was so overcome by the idea of becoming Sigmund's successor, she had almost forgotten to whom she was telling her sinister secrets.

"Sigmund, you tricked me!" Meevillain shrieked. "I will only give you *my* secret antidote if you agree that I will become the king's royal wizard when you die. In return for your agreement, I will tell you *my* secret ingredients to make the antidote for *my* powerful nuptial nectar that made the king and queen childless!"

"Listen carefully," Meevillain said to Sigmund. "The king and queen will have to risk their lives and give up something of themselves for *my* antidote to work. *My* magical antidote will only be enough for one pregnancy, a girl child. But this girl child will only be healthy until her fifth birthday, and then she will become gravely ill. Every day she will sleep for a longer time until she falls into a never-ending sleep."

Sigmund was shocked by Meevillain's evilness, but he knew that with her magical antidote the king and queen could have the joyful blessing of a child, even if only for a short time. He turned away from Meevillain for a moment to think and said to himself, "I am heartbroken by this news, but I will carry the secret of the baby's future deep within my heart so as not to worry the king and queen. Meevillain knows that I am King Alexander's trusted confidant and faithful friend, that I would give my life for the royal couple. I must agree to Meevillain's wickedness and spare my beloved king and queen deeper sadness. At last they will have the joyful blessing of a child, and I will have five years to find a cure for the never-ending sleeping sickness."

With mixed emotions and a deep awareness of the consequences of her antidote, Sigmund said, "Meevillain, I will agree to your insidious plan because I know how devoted the king and queen are to one another. I am certain they will unselfishly be willing to risk their lives to share the joyful blessing of a child."

Suddenly, Sigmund felt the chilling wind whirling around him again. "I am exhausted. I must sit down and rest again before returning to the royal castle," Sigmund said weakly.

"Sigmund, take hold of my staff and I will help you sit down," Meevillain said. At the very moment that Sigmund touched Meevillain's staff, he fell into a deep sleep. All his memory of where the Forest of Fear was located was erased. But Meevillain's foretelling of the princess's illness and the ingredients for Meevillain's antidote remained deep in his heart and mind.

As Sigmund slept, Meevillain proclaimed, "I will safeguard my future powers with a sinister spell. An ominous Cloud of Chaos will shadow the entire kingdom. My cloud will transform the Kingdom of Kindness into the Kingdom of Intolerance and Misunderstanding. My sinister spell will begin on the second day of the second month of the new year, when the queen gives birth to the long-awaited princess. After the princess is born, the villagers will gradually change their attitudes about themselves and each other. No one will notice at first, but through the years the villagers will become less tolerant and understanding of each other's differences. Where there had once been open acceptance and respect for one another, the villagers will build walls of mistrust and misunderstanding between the villages."

Sigmund awakened from his solemn slumber and slowly began his journey back to the royal castle. On his return, he told the royal couple, "I found Meevillain! She was in her Forest of Fear that she created in the Forest of Friendship. I have also learned the secret ingredients to make the antidote for her nuptial nectar."

It was springtime. King Alexander and Queen Sylvia were enjoying the delicate sweet-scented flowers of the Garden of Knowledge and the abundant healing herbs that bloomed in the fields surrounding the royal castle. As in years past, they joyfully shared the fruits of their labor with all the villagers and visitors from distant lands.

It was from the aromatic garden and blooming fields that Sigmund found the ingredients for the antidote. He created Queen Sylvia's pregnancy potion from eight

magic mushrooms, six green healing herbs, two yellow
sunflowers, four orange tiger lilies, five blue
forget-me-nots, plus one lily of the valley.

"My dear friends, you must demonstrate
the highest level of trust for my healing
powers. The pregnancy potion will only
be effective if you, King Alexander, will
give part of your heart to give your child
the spirit of love. And, Queen Sylvia, you
must give a lobe from one of your lungs to
provide your child with the breath of life,"
Sigmund explained.

Without hesitating a moment,
they agreed and said, "Sigmund,
of course, we trust
you and your healing
powers."

"I must put you both into
a deep sleep. When you
awaken, you will have the child your
hearts desire, but you will never again
rejoice in perfect health," he told them.

"We are willing to risk our lives, and we understand the
consequences," the royal couple said without hesitation.

On the first night of the full moon and every night thereafter, the king and queen
drank the pregnancy potion. When Queen Sylvia became very uncomfortable and
suffered sickness every morning, she knew these were signs of her pregnancy. The
king and queen were ecstatic.

Nine months later, on the second day of the second month of the new year, the
day the folk tale says the ground hog comes out of hibernation to look for his
shadow, Queen Sylvia gave birth to a baby girl.

At the very moment the baby princess was born, the winter's sun began to shine
brightly and the lilies of the valley bloomed. But, strangely, the ground hog did not
see his shadow, for an ominous cloud began to shadow the Kingdom of Kindness
and the bright sunshine.

*You will find reflections about this chapter
on page 105 of the* Gift Giver's Guide.

Precious Gifts

When their daughter was eight days old, King Alexander and Queen Sylvia hosted a traditional baby-naming celebration. To show their gratitude, the royal couple gave Sigmund the honor of choosing a name for their daughter. Sigmund said, "I give your daughter the name, Shayna, which means beautiful in my ancient Cush language. Princess Shayna is a beautiful, precious gift to all of us and to our kingdom," he said proudly.

The entire kingdom rejoiced with jubilation for their beloved king and queen. Many honored guests came to the royal baby-naming celebration. They all brought exquisite gifts and blessings for Princess Shayna. As the king and queen celebrated in the royal castle, the villagers were busy planting celebration gardens in their villages. The villagers planted many new varieties of yellow sunflowers, blue forget-me-nots, orange tiger lilies and green healing herbs—the flowers and healing herbs that Sigmund used in the antidote pregnancy potion.

When Princess Shayna was born, the royal couple asked Queen Sylvia's parents, Lord Harry and Lady Eva, to move from the Village of the Yellow Sunflowers and live in the royal castle with them. They wanted Princess Shayna to have the special love and wisdom only her grandparents could give her.

Lady Eva baked delicious pastries in honor of her granddaughter's birth and served them at the celebration. "These little crescent-shaped cinnamon cakes are the queen's favorite pastries. Their spicy aroma has filled every nook and cranny of the royal

11

castle. These gifts symbolize a sweet life for Princess Shayna," Lord Harry and Lady Eva said.

Lord Harry and Lady Eva also gave the baby princess a pair of ornate silver candles that were embossed with delicate flowers. "One candle represents wisdom, and the other candle represents peace. An ancient blessing of thanksgiving also accompanies these candles. They will always illuminate Princess Shayna's journey through life. All she will have to do is circle her hands over the candles three times, and they will illuminate her path," Lady Eva said.

Lord Markus, from the Village of the Green Healing Herbs, brought Princess Shayna a kaleidoscope filled with priceless blue, yellow, green, and orange sapphires. Lord Markus had carefully carved the kaleidoscope himself from the satinwood trees that surrounded his castle. "Princess Shayna can always carry this ever-changing gift with her. It will teach her to be responsible for the changes in her life. It is a symbol of the unique gift the princess will possess, the ability to recognize and appreciate the strengths and differences in other people," he foretold.

Lord John and Lady Michelle from the Village of the Blue Forget-Me-Nots brought Princess Shayna two extraordinary gifts. The first was an intuition compass made especially for the princess. "There is no other compass like this. When Princess Shayna holds it, the spinning silver needle will point to miniature paintings of the villages—north to the Village of the Yellow Sunflowers, south to the Village of the Orange Tiger Lilies, east to the Village of the Blue Forget-Me-Nots, or west to the Village of the Green Healing Herbs. Her intuition compass will give her self-direction. It also represents her ability to follow her heart and soul when making decisions that will affect herself and others," they said.

The second gift Lord John and Lady Michele brought was a resonating seashell from the long island on which they had once lived. "Our seashell will teach Princess Shayna to listen to and be respectful of other people, even if they are very different from her. The compass and seashell will give her the treasured gift of true friendship," they explained.

Lord Joseph and Lady Lillian came from the Village of the Orange Tiger Lilies. Lord Joseph, the king's royal falconer said, "We have brought Princess Shayna a perfect white falcon with inquisitive tourmaline eyes. Two years before the princess was born, this rare creature was hatched. As the falcon matured, his perfect white feathers remained. No one had ever seen a pure white falcon before."

"While we were raising and training the white falcon, we realized that he possessed special intuitive powers. When the little princess was born, we knew why we had been blessed with the caring and training of such a peerless bird. He is our most praiseworthy and precious gift, our most prized possession that we lovingly give to Princess Shayna," they said proudly.

"The white falcon will always be Princess Shayna's beloved and devoted companion and share three unique gifts with her. The first gift will be acute vision to comprehend the world around her. The second gift will be guidance to help her rise above any difficulties in her life. The third gift will be courage to meet life's challenges and turn her obstacles into opportunities," Lord Joseph and Lady Lillian proclaimed.

From the moment Lord Joseph perched the white falcon on Princess Shayna's royal cradle, the rare raptor was completely devoted to his beloved princess. He watched over her day and night. The white falcon could sense the baby princess's unspoken thoughts and needs. Princess Shayna and the white falcon seemed to speak to each other even before the baby princess could talk.

The king told Queen Sylvia confidently, "I know we never need worry about Princess Shayna, for the white falcon will always watch over our daughter. He will be her beloved and devoted life-long companion."

As the baby-naming celebration was coming to a close, Jani the Queen of the Flower Fairies, who lived in the pink magnolia trees surrounding the Garden of Knowledge, appeared. She was wearing a dress made from silken silver spider threads that Sarah Spundah, the silver spider and guardian of the Forest of Friendship, had spun for her. A garland of yellow sunflowers, blue forget-me-nots, orange tiger lilies and green healing herbs adorned her flowing chestnut hair.

Jani said, "I have also brought a praiseworthy gift, but it is for the king and queen. It is a 'love gift' they will continue to give Princess Shayna all her life. The gift will be invisible, but when King Alexander and Queen Sylvia share it with their daughter, it will become visible upon her. This Invisible Visible Gift is a fragile circle of life, like the garland of flowers that I wear. This valuable gift cannot be bought, sold, or taken from Princess Shayna. She will joyfully share this gift with others, but only if they will truly accept it. And it will only become visible upon them if they will share the Invisible Visible Gift with others."

You will find reflections about this chapter on page 106 of the Gift Giver's Guide.

14

Silver Apricots

While everyone in the kingdom was rejoicing, Meevillain was celebrating the creation of her ominous Cloud of Chaos that had begun to shadow the entire kingdom. "My Cloud of Chaos will cause great unhappiness and misunderstanding in every village of the kingdom. The king and queen will try everything within their power to help their villagers. Their royal advisors will spend many sleepless nights trying to figure out the cause of my Cloud of Chaos, and Sigmund the Royal Wizard will try magic potions, but all will be in vain," she promised.

Although Meevillain's Cloud of Chaos began to create a great discomfort within the kingdom, Princess Shayna always felt happy and safe. The king and queen were very grateful for their gift, Princess Shayna, who always brought laughter and joy to everyone in the kingdom. Then, during the night after her fifth birthday celebration, Princess Shayna became gravely ill. "I am bewildered by her illness and frightened with the thought of losing our precious gift. We must awaken Sigmund, immediately! You know he loves our daughter as his own and would give his life for hers," the queen told the king.

Sigmund was summoned to the princess's royal bedchamber, where the white falcon and Princess Shayna's parents were watching over her. With a great sense of relief and despair, Sigmund knew he must tell the royal family the complete truth about his agreement with Meevillain.

"I had hoped this time would never come," Sigmund said sadly. "I can no longer carry the secret of Princess Shayna's future deep within my heart. Now I must tell you the whole truth." And he told the king and queen about how Meevillain had cast a spell on the little princess.

"Sigmund, we understand. Your love and devotion to us caused you to make your agreement with Meevillain. Remember, if you had not, we would not have our precious gift, Princess Shayna," the king and queen said. "We have confidence that you can create a solution to our problem, as you always have!"

For many months Sigmund kept a vigil at Princess Shayna's bedside. When he was not with her, he was creating different magic potions to help the princess feel better. "I will taste the magic potion first," he would say to the little princess. His gentleness always made her feel safe and secure. "Shayna, I love you as if you were my own child. I am trying my very best to make you well," he would say.

"Thank you, Sigi, my royal wizard," Princess Shayna would answer affectionately, "I love you more than tongue can tell!"

Sigmund was becoming very discouraged that Princess Shayna continued to be ill and slept longer and longer each day. One afternoon he decided to take a walk and contemplate a cure for Princess Shayna's illness. As the full moon was rising, he finally stopped to rest under one of the ancient ginkgo trees King Alexander's grandfather had planted when he had built the royal castle.

The ginkgo trees were planted as a symbol of longevity and survival for the Kingdom of Kindness. They had been given to the king's grandfather as a gift from a visitor from a distant land far to the east. The ancient ginkgo trees had just finished blooming their golden flowers, and the sparkling silver apricots remained on their uplifting branches. As Sigmund leaned against the sturdy trunk of the ancient tree, the delicate fan-shaped leaflets gently soothed his tired body. Just as he was about to fall asleep, a familiar chilling wind began to whirl around him. "I must return to the castle immediately. I can rest my old bones after I have checked on Princess Shayna," he said to himself. Sigmund reached for a tree limb to support himself. As he did, a silver apricot fell to the ground and broke open. A strange aroma and silver white fluid flowed from the shattered fruit.

"Rimsiyavyo!" Sigmund exclaimed in his ancient Cush language. "This is the answer. I now remember! When I was a young man in Cush, my wise teacher told me that the milky liquid from silver apricots often was used to cure lingering sleeping illnesses. "This is the cure I have been looking for. Rimsiyavyo!" he shouted.

Sigmund quickly plucked more silver apricots from the ancient ginkgo tree. Then he hurried back to the castle as fast as his antiquated legs could carry him. "I will not rest until I have made a magic potion to help Princess Shayna," he said with great commitment.

By morning, all his tests had proven to be successful. "Rimsiyavyo! I will give the princess a taste before her breakfast," he joyfully said to himself.

Sarah Spundah, who had been sleeping in one of her beautiful silver spider webs in the window of Sigmund's royal chamber was abruptly awakened by Sigmund's joyful exclamations. "Sarah, would you please spin your silken spider threads into a container to hold Princess Shayna's silver apricot potion?" Sigmund asked.

"It will be my pleasure to help the little princess," Sarah Spundah replied. And she quickly spun a small silver bottle that looked exactly like the silver apricots that hung on the ancient ginkgo tree.

"Thank you, Sarah. This is perfect!" Sigmund said as he rushed off to Princess Shayna's royal bedchamber.

The princess and her parents were about to have their favorite breakfast of Lady Eva's freshly baked cinnamon cakes as Sigmund dashed into her royal bedchamber.

"Good morning, Sigi," Princess Shayna said.

"It is a glorious morning, indeed, for I have discovered a cure for your illness, Princess Shayna," Sigmund replied joyfully.

"Rimsiyavyo!" the royal family said in unison, and the white falcon flapped his wings with excitement.

"Your magic silver apricot potion is stored in this silver bottle that Sarah Spundah spun for you," Sigmund told her. "Princess Shayna, listen carefully to my instructions. First, you must always carry your magic potion with you wherever you go. Second, this silver apricot-shaped bottle will always refill itself, all you have to do is turn it upside down and three little droplets will be released onto your fingertips. Third, and most important, you must faithfully take the silver apricot potion before you eat. You must promise to perform your new routine faithfully. If you do not dispense your silver apricot potion as I have instructed, you will become gravely ill again, and you will fall into a never-ending sleep." Sigmund said lovingly, but firmly.

Princess Shayna learned to dispense her silver apricot potion at the appropriate times and quickly regained her good health. Handling her illness could have been a difficult task for the princess. But, with the white falcon, her family's love and her Invisible Visible Gift, she responded enthusiastically to her new routine. She learned to meet the challenge of her illness. She turned what could have been an obstacle into an opportunity to understand others who also had to overcome difficulties in their lives. Princess Shayna also developed a great sense of empathy and an appreciation of life and its blessings of good health and comfort.

You will find reflections about this chapter
on page 107 of the Gift Giver's Guide.

Princess Shayna

Early in Princess Shayna's childhood she became aware that her parents did not have perfect health. When she asked them why they became ill, they told her the truth about the sacrifices they had made to give her life.

The king and queen were always able to comfort and calm their daughter by telling her stories. Her favorite story was about her parents' great happiness when she was born. She loved to hear what a special gift she was and how much they loved her.

"Please tell me how Mother drank the magic pregnancy potion Sigi made and how happy you were when you received the special gift you wanted most. Me!" Princess Shayna would exclaim.

King Alexander and Queen Sylvia always set definite times in their busy royal schedules to spend time alone with Princess Shayna. She loved creating and sharing her own traditions with each of her parents. Every day the queen read stories to her daughter. Their favorite reading time was in her parents' royal bedchamber. They snuggled up together in the cold of winter on the queen's cozy down-filled chair next to the warmth of the fire in the large marble fireplace. And she enjoyed baking Lady Eva's delicate pastries in the royal kitchen with her mother and grandmother.

Princess Shayna also loved playing with the many beautiful dolls that visitors from distant lands brought her. The queen had taught Princess Shayna the pleasure of reading books and the joy of creating and using her imagination. Most importantly, Queen Sylvia always told her daughter, "I am very proud of you, and I love you very much."

"I always feel happy and good about myself when you tell me you love me," Princess Shayna would reply.

Each day the king and the princess read quietly together, and they often went horseback riding or practiced archery. The princess loved to read in the king's royal library in his oversized chair or under one of the ancient ginkgo trees.

But, most of all, the little princess loved to accompany her father to the royal chapel that King Alexander had built and proclaimed open to all the villagers and visitors from distant lands. Princess Shayna and the king would sit together in the last row of the chapel. "Father, I love to listen to you chant your daily prayers and sing off key," she would giggle.

The princess learned to laugh silently at her father's singing ability so as not to disturb him. King Alexander was a very pious man and would lovingly scold the little princess when she asked him too many questions instead of listening, or when she braided the fringes on his prayer shawl. He was always very patient with her and encouraged her thirst for knowledge and her desire to seek new challenges. Most importantly, the king often told his daughter, "I am very proud of you, and I love you very much."

"I always feel happy and good about myself when you tell me you love me," Princess Shayna would reply.

It would be these special times with her parents that the princess would draw upon for strength in her life. It was their love and the Invisible Visible Gift they shared that gave her a balanced perspective of life.

Princess Shayna also enjoyed spending time alone in her royal bedchamber. Sarah Spundah had spun a silver cradle for her when she was born. It was a perfect place for the white falcon to perch while he kept watch over his beloved princess.

When Princess Shayna grew too big for the silver cradle, her parents had a two-poster bed carved for their daughter. A delicately curved canopy covered the princess's head and protected her from the mysterious chilling wind that occasionally swept through the castle. Princess Shayna loved to read and play dolls on her bed, and it became another favorite perch for the white falcon.

Princess Shayna loved the clothes that her mother and grandmother made for her dolls. Many visitors from distant lands brought her dolls dressed in their traditional costumes. Princess Shayna was always curious to see how different the doll's features and costumes were from one another.

King Alexander and Queen Sylvia taught their daughter to respect and accept other people's differences. "After all, being a princess, having red hair, and needing to take your apricot potion makes you different, too," they would tell her.

Princess Shayna was a very creative child with a wonderful imagination. Pretending was one of her favorite pastimes. She was content to play school, house or the queen with her dolls. She loved reading to her dolls and teaching them how to solve their problems. Her playfulness delighted everyone in the castle. They all helped to nurture and encourage the young princess because they knew that someday her pretend adventures could become her reality.

Everyone in the castle also marveled at Princess Shayna's conversations with the white falcon. Of course, they thought their conversations were part of her imagination, too, but that was not so.

When Princess Shayna was a small child, the white falcon began to perch on her right shoulder and put his head next to her ear. Everyone thought he was being affectionate, but he was really sharing his thoughts with her.

One day when the princess was talking to the white falcon, he said. "I love you more than tongue can tell, and I have been waiting for the right time to tell you that I understand you. But you are the only person that can hear me."

"Oh, White Falcon, I love you more than tongue can tell," Princess Shayna responded, looking directly into his inquisitive tourmaline eyes.

To prepare the princess for her future, the king and queen wanted their daughter to be tutored in the lessons appropriate for a young princess. They had heard stories about a remarkable woman who was totally devoted to all her students. When the royal family finally met this woman, they immediately knew she was the perfect teacher for Princess Shayna. Her name was Macdolodge, and she was a delightful women, diminutive in stature but lofty in experience. She quickly became completely dedicated to Princess Shayna.

Mac, as Princess Shayna affectionately called her, told the king and queen, "I would like Princess Shayna to share her academic lessons with the children from the four villages. I will invite the children to study and play with your daughter. They all will learn valuable lessons about cooperation and good sportsmanship. They will also learn to respect the many gifts of the living world that surrounds them."

Mac was a sensitive teacher and an encouraging mentor for the young princess. Princess Shayna also shared Mac's love for poetry. After a day of study and play, the princess would often say, "Mac, please recite a poem from your little blue book." Mac was a wise tutor because she would explain how the poetry related to the lessons she had diligently taught the children.

As the princess grew from a child into a young girl, she was really quite unaware and unaffected by her loveliness or the manner in which she was accustomed to living. She did not desire material possessions or the beautiful clothes that most young princesses of her age adored. Her greatest desire was for her parents to enjoy good health.

Because of her family life, Princess Shayna developed a great insight into other people. She could see what others could not see in themselves. She could show people their strengths and their gifts! The princess honored everyone, no matter what their job or position in the kingdom. Her words of wisdom enlightened people's souls and lightened their burdens in life. To them, her words were more precious than the jewels in her kaleidoscope. Princess Shayna truly possessed and demonstrated many admirable attributes and abilities to someday guide and care for the Kingdom of Kindness.

You will find reflections about this chapter
on page 108 of the Gift Giver's Guide.

Vision Quest

The time had come to prepare Princess Shayna for her royal responsibilities as the future queen of the kingdom. The four royal advisors expressed their concerns about how Princess Shayna would someday care for and guide the kingdom.

The royal advisor from the Village of the Yellow Sunflowers said, "Princess Shayna has never been outside the castle walls for a long period of time. She has enjoyed studying and playing with the village children, but she has not spent enough time in the four villages to understand the children and their families. She must learn to recognize and respect their differences and similarities."

The king and queen listened to the royal advisor and agreed that it was time to prepare a plan for Princess Shayna's traditional rites of passage that would prepare her for her royal responsibilities as the future queen of the kingdom.

King Alexander was known for his trustworthiness and wisdom, and Queen Sylvia for her compassion and thoughtfulness. Listening to others created a great sense of comfort and respectfulness toward everyone in their kingdom. The king and queen were also very insightful and valued other people's perspectives, as well as their child's. Even when Princess Shayna was a small child, her parents asked her to share her ideas and feelings with them.

King Alexander told Queen Sylvia, "I think the time has come to ask Princess Shayna what she thinks she should do to prove herself worthy of the responsibilities as the future queen of the kingdom."

Queen Sylvia agreed and said, "I think we should summon our royal advisors to the garden today, where we all can listen to Princess Shayna's ideas."

That afternoon everyone assembled under the honey locust tree. Princess Shayna entered the garden with White Falcon perched upon her shoulder. Her enthusiasm immediately filled the entire garden. She kissed her parents "good afternoon" and wiggled herself between them, as she had often done since she was a small child.

After Princess Shayna stopped wiggling, King Alexander said, "Shayna, we would like to hear how you think you should prove yourself worthy of the responsibilities as the future queen of the Kingdom of Kindness."

Princess Shayna thought for a while and then said, "I have observed many interesting changes in the villagers' behaviors whenever someone from another village comes to the castle. At first, new arrivals feel uncomfortable, cautious and suspicious of those from other villages. They are extremely critical of their differences—how they talk, eat, dance, play, sing, make decisions, and their entire attitude toward life. Then, after some time, the different villagers become more comfortable with one another and enjoy learning and working together. And, when it's time for the visitors to return to their own villages, they are unhappy because they will no longer see their new friends. The walls around their villages will keep them from learning and sharing with each other, as they did in the castle."

Everyone had listened carefully while Princess Shayna spoke. Then the royal advisor from the Village of the Blue Forget-Me-Nots said, "I remember many years ago, when the four villages of the Kingdom of Kindness had a strong sense of community and respect for one another. As I remember, it was the year Princess Shayna was born that the ominous dark cloud began to shadow all our villages. In time, all the villagers built stone walls around their villages. They never worked or played with one another again."

"You four royal advisors are the only exceptions. I had asked you to serve in the royal court before the princess's birth. The dark cloud is a very strange and sad puzzlement that no one has been able to solve," King Alexander explained.

Princess Shayna exclaimed enthusiastically, "Rimsiyavyo! That will be my Vision Quest! I will journey to each of the four villages and learn their perspectives and lifestyles. From each village, I will glean the wisdom I will need to become queen. I know that I can help the villagers to live and work together again!"

"That is a splendid idea," said the royal advisor from the Village of the Orange Tiger Lilies. "But, I think you also need to return with a special gift from each village—a gift to prove that each village has accepted you into its community."

"An emissary from each village should accompany you home. The emissaries will verify that you have learned the unique lessons you will need to guide and care for the kingdom," said the royal advisory from the Village of the Blue Forget-Me-Nots.

"Princess Shayna, your rite of passage shall begin on the second day of the second month of the new year. Before you begin, on your thirteenth birthday, there will be an ancient ceremony. This event will mark the beginning of your Vision Quest to prove you are capable and worthy of becoming the queen of the Kingdom of Kindness!" said the royal advisor from the Village of the Yellow Sunflowers.

"Your Vision Quest will last for one year and must be completed on the second day of the second month of the new year," said the royal advisor from the Village of the Green Healing Herbs.

"We all agree!" the royal advisors said unanimously.

The royal advisor from the Village of the Yellow Sunflowers said, "Princess Shayna, you will travel to my village where many varieties of yellow sunflowers were planted in honor of your birth. There you will learn to understand and value the true meaning of dependability, loyalty, preparation, and commitment."

The royal advisor from the Village of the Blue Forget-Me-Nots said, "Princess Shayna, you will travel to my village where many varieties of blue forget-me-nots were planted to honor your birth. There you will learn to understand and value the true meaning of helpfulness, friendship, compassion, and respect for the land's natural wonders."

The royal advisor from the Village of the Orange Tiger Lilies said, "Princess Shayna, you will travel to my village where many varieties of orange tiger lilies were planted in honor of your birth. There, you will learn to understand and value the true meaning of courage, resourcefulness, open-mindedness, and the vitality of life."

The royal advisor from the Village of the Green Healing Herbs said, "Princess Shayna, you will travel to my village where many varieties of green healing herbs were planted to honor your birth. There you will learn to understand and value the true meaning of logical thinking, individuality, justice, and the joy of seeking knowledge."

In unison, the royal advisors said, "Princess Shayna, you must use your Invisible Visible Gift to help the people of each village recognize and understand each other's perspectives and help them to work together again."

King Alexander immediately accepted the plan that he knew would be very challenging for his daughter. However, Queen Sylvia said hesitantly, "I will worry and fear for our daughter's well-being. She will have to leave the safety of the royal castle and journey through the Forest of Friendship, and possibly venture into Meevillain's Forest of Fear!

"We all know the legend that within the Forest of Friendship is a menacing Forest of Fear that no one dares to venture into. Only Sigmund has been there and returned to tell the tale. But Meevillain cast a magic spell over him that erased any memory of the location of her Forest of Fear," the queen said.

King Alexander gently comforted Queen Sylvia and said, "My dear, we have given our daughter the strength of our love and her Invisible Visible Gift. Remember, we have always taught Princess Shayna to face her fears."

"I agree to the requirements of the challenge," Princes Shayna said confidently. "I am so excited and grateful that you all respect and share my vision. Thank you for understanding my passion and commitment to demonstrate my worthiness to someday become queen. I know deep in my heart that I am capable of such a challenge.

"Mother, White Falcon will accompany me on my Vision Quest. He will protect me," Princess Shayna added. "Now I must take the first step on my Vision Quest and prepare for what will be one of the greatest adventures of my life!"

The next morning while Princess Shayna was finishing her preparations for her Vision Quest, there was a knock at the door of her royal bedchamber. She ran to the door to see who was there. To her delight, it was her grandparents.

Princess Shayna always enjoyed spending time with her grandparents. They made her feel loved and secure, and she dearly loved them. Mimi and Poppy, as Princess Shayna affectionately called them, had come to spend time with her while she prepared for her Vision Quest. Poppy said, "Princess Shayna, remember how much you love playing our string game made from Sarah Spundah's silken spider threads?"

"Yes, Poppy," said Princess Shayna. "Our favorite game taught me to be patient and how to create strategies to solve my problems and make good decisions in my life. Now I will use those skills for my Vision Quest."

Poppy said, "You know I am very proud of you and love you very much. I have a special 'love gift' for you to take on your Vision Quest. Guess which hand it is in!"

"The right one," Princess Shayna said confidently.

Poppy slowly opened his right hand to reveal a small amethyst-colored velvet bag that was a magnificent shade of purple just like the royal irises that bloomed in the Garden of Knowledge. "Inside this bag, there are 365 little seed pearls and a beautiful golden necklace that has a special lock to let you thread a new pearl on your necklace each day. Use it to count each day of your Vision Quest. Remember you must keep your agreement and return home on the second day of the second month of the new year," Poppy advised.

"Oh, thank you so much, Poppy. It is beautiful, and I will remember!" Princess Shayna said as her grandfather hugged her close to his heart.

Mimi said, "You know I am very proud of you and love you very much. I, too, have a special 'love gift' for you to take on your Vision Quest." Mimi gave Princess Shayna a white organdy pinafore and said, "This magical pinafore will protect you, my cherished granddaughter. It has many heart-shaped pockets trimmed in white eyelet, and each pocket is filled with love. The magical pinafore's protective power will help you carry your many childhood treasures on your Vision Quest. Each heart-shaped pocket's love will transform a treasure to fit inside it. When you take your treasure out of its pocket, the pocket's love will transform your treasure back to its original size and number. And if you desire another heart-shaped pocket, it will appear as you need it. You will have many gifts to carry on your journey, but they will not become a burden because of the love that fills each pocket!"

"Oh, thank you so much, Mimi. It is beautiful!" Princess Shayna said as her grandmother hugged her close to her heart.

"Mimi, I would love to see the magical pinafore work!" the young princess said curiously.

"Of course, you can, my child," her grandmother encouraged.

"In this heart-shaped pocket, I will put one of my delicious cinnamon cakes. Look! As I remove it from the heart-shaped pocket, another little cake appears!" Mimi said.

"Your pastries will sustain me on my journey and remind me of your gentleness," Princess Shayna said.

"Watch! This heart-shaped pocket will transform the silver candles that carry my blessings of wisdom and peace," said Mimi.

"I know your candles will help illuminate my path on my Vision Quest," Princess Shayna said.

"And the love inside this heart-shaped pocket transformed the kaleidoscope that Lord Markus gave me. Its ever-changing patterns will remind me that I am responsible for all the changes in my life. It will also help me to recognize and appreciate the strengths and differences in people I will meet in the different villages.

"My magical pinafore has two connecting heart-shaped pockets. Look! The seashell is becoming smaller and smaller to fit into one of the connecting pockets. Lord John and Lady Michelle's seashell will help me to listen to and be respectful of the people I will meet, even if they are very different than I am. The other connecting pocket is for my intuition compass, which will give me self-direction and help me follow my heart and soul when making decisions. I know these two gifts will be a comfort to me because they represent the blessing of true friendship.

"Mimi, I do not see a pocket for my purple velvet bag of add-a-pearls, and I also will need a pocket for my silver apricot," Princess Shayna observed.

"Just as you wish, my child," Mimi said confidently.

As Mimi spoke, two new heart-shaped pockets appeared on the magical pinafore—one for Princess Shayna's add-a-pearls and one for her silver apricot.

There was another knock at the door. It was Mac! "I have written all your favorite poems in this little book," Mac said. Princess Shayna gently ran her hands over her book. On the blue leather cover, inlaid in gold, were the words, *It Can Be Done*.

"These inspiring words will remind you of the confidence I have in your abilities," Mac said as she hugged Princess Shayna close to her heart.

"Oh, thank you, Mac." Princess Shayna said gratefully. "I know your poetry will inspire me on my Vision Quest. Now I will need another pocket for my poetry book," she said excitedly. As quickly as the princess spoke, her poetry book became smaller and fit perfectly into the new heart-shaped pocket that appeared on her magical pinafore.

A few days before Princess Shayna's birthday celebration, Queen Sylvia came to her daughter's royal bedchamber, "I have a special gift for you, my precious child. I have sewn and embroidered this celebration dress for you. This special fabric is the color of green healing herbs and is embroidered with yellow sunflowers, blue forget-me-nots, and orange tiger lilies to represent the four villages of the Kingdom of Kindness."

"Thank you very much, Mother. I know you are concerned about me, but do not worry. You and Father have given me the strength of your love and my Invisible

Visible Gift. Remember, you have always taught me to face my fears," Princess Shayna said as her mother hugged her close to her heart.

The traditional ancient rite of passage celebration was conducted on the morning of Princess Shayna's thirteenth birthday, which was the second day of the second month of the new year. With White Falcon perched proudly on Princess Shayna's shoulder, she accompanied her parents, Mimi, Poppy, Lord Markus, Lord Joseph, Lady Lillian, Lord John, Lady Michele, Sigmund the Royal Wizard, Mac, and the royal advisors to the royal chapel. Even Jani the Queen of the Flower Fairies and Sarah Spundah the Silver Spider came to the chapel.

Princess Shayna observed an ancient custom of reading from the books that told of her family's heritage. She had even prepared a special speech to close the ceremony. She said, "Now I know I am considered a woman who is responsible for faithfully keeping the teachings and customs of my ancient heritage. I know you all are very proud of me. As my mother and grandmother before me, I will strive to become a responsible woman—a Woman of Valor."

*You will find reflections about this chapter
on page 109 of the* Gift Giver's Guide.

Into the Forest

On the afternoon of the second day of second month of the new year, Princess Shayna kissed all her loved ones farewell. She walked down the stone path that led through the peaceful Garden of Knowledge toward the large courtyard gate.

Sigmund accompanied Princess Shayna as she walked through the garden to meet her father. "Princess Shayna, your life will be very different while you are on your Vision Quest. You must remember all my instructions about your silver apricot potion," Sigmund warned Princess Shayna as he hugged her close to his heart.

"Thank you for your concern, Sigi. Don't worry, I will remember everything you have told me," Princess Shayna pledged as she waved good-bye.

"I am so grateful for everyone's love and concern," Princess Shayna said to White Falcon as they walked through the garden to meet the king.

"And you know I will always be here to protect you," White Falcon said softly.

It was agreed that King Alexander would meet Princess Shayna at the large green gate that led northward out from the shelter of the peaceful Garden of Knowledge and into the Forest of Friendship. When Princess Shayna arrived at the gate, her father was waiting for her. "You have received many gifts for your Vision Quest. I can only give you the knowledge that I have confidence in you, my child. Know that I will always be by your side. Take this map of the kingdom. I trust that you will create your own paths, make your choices, and face your fears. You must remember to remain alert and beware of Meevillain's Forest of Fear, for no one knows exactly where it is located," the king cautioned as he hugged his daughter close to his heart.

Then Princess Shayna kissed King Alexander on both cheeks, a tradition she had created whenever he traveled from the royal castle. "Thank you for your confidence in me, Father. I will be careful." Princess Shayna promised.

She checked all her belongings and perched White Falcon on her shoulder. She stepped upon the stone threshold in front of the large green courtyard gate that led from the shelter of the peaceful Garden of Knowledge, placed both her hands on the large iron lock, unlatched the gate and began her Vision Quest—one that would take her and White Falcon into the Forest of Friendship and, hopefully, not into the Forest of Fear.

As King Alexander watched Princess Shayna leave the safety of the royal castle's ivy-covered walls, he rejoiced in her enthusiasm for her journey, for that was how she always approached life!

Princess Shayna paused a moment to watch her father close the gate. When she heard him latch the gate that protected her many childhood memories, Princess Shayna said to herself, "Now I understand why I must make my Vision Quest alone."

Deep in her Forest of Fear, Meevillain was also celebrating because her Cloud of Chaos that cast its ominous shadow upon the kingdom was growing larger and larger. Meevillain said, "I will make sure Princess Shayna will never complete her Vision Quest. Then I will become the royal wizard, for Sigmund is well beyond his 120th year and will surely die of a broken heart. When my wicked wind has blown through Princess Shayna's royal bedchamber, I have heard Sigmund tell the princess that he loves her like his own child."

So that she could follow Princess Shayna, Meevillain transformed herself into a raven and flew off toward her Forest of Fear. She said, "At the edge of my Forest of Fear, I will find the greedy and treacherous trolls that live in the pool of slime under the largest moss-covered rock. I will transform them to look like royal woodsmen of the Forest of Friendship."

Meevillain's Forest of Fear contained not one living creature except for the greedy, treacherous trolls. Every single tree, plant, and flower was dead. All the tree trunks were twisted and contorted. The paths were crooked and went in circles and led nowhere!

Raven Meevillain said, "I will transform one greedy and treacherous troll to look like the head woodsman of the Forest of Friendship and name him Mennis. Then I will transform the other troll into Mennis's lackey and name him Meene."

Meevillain found the trolls sleeping in the pool of slime under the large moss-covered rock. "Crawl out of your pool of slime, you deceitful duo," she commanded.

The pair quickly emerged, trying to wipe off the slime. "Stop trying to clean yourselves off and listen closely to what I am going to tell you. I will transform you into the royal woodsmen of the Forest of Friendship. Then I want you to deceive and confuse Princess Shayna so she will not complete her Vision Quest and return home safely. When you complete your treacherous task, Sigmund the Royal Wizard will surely die of a broken heart and I will become the royal wizard," Meevillain exclaimed. "Then I will be able to transform the entire Kingdom of Kindness into my Kingdom of Chaos. I will become so powerful that King Alexander will give the entire Forest of Friendship to me. In return for your loyalty to me, I will convert the entire Forest of Friendship into my Forest of Fear and give total control and power over the entire Forest of Fear to you," Meevillain promised.

Immediately, Mennis and Meene's greedy little minds envisioned control of the entire Forest of Friendship. "We will be able to keep all the villagers from entering and enjoying the forest. We will control the entire Forest of Friendship when Meevillain converts it into her Forest of Fear. We will have it all for ourselves," they said greedily.

Raven Meevillain, Mennis, and Meene began to plot their sinister scheme to deceive Princess Shayna. Then Meevillain took flight to follow Princess Shayna on her Vision Quest, and the treacherous trolls began to celebrate by drinking the magic power potion Meevillain left for them. Mennis and Meene became so drunk with power that they fell into a sinister slumber and were blanketed by the ominous shadow from the Cloud of Chaos that had expanded over the kingdom.

As Princess Shayna was about to enter the Forest of Friendship, she noticed a sense of dreadful darkness shadowing her path. She dismissed her uncomfortable feelings and attributed the darkness to the lush green canopy made by the beautiful foliage of the Forest of Friendship. As she approached the entrance to the forest she heard a familiar sweet song being sung.

"Sarah Spundah, Sarah Spundah, Sarah Spundah rat, tat, tat.
Sarah Spundah, Sarah Spundah, Sarah Spundah, a lacy web of life I spin!
Sarah Spundah, Sarah Spundah, Sarah Spundah rat, tat, tat.
Sarah Spundah, Sarah Spundah, Sarah Spundah, a lacy web of life I weave!"

Princess Shayna looked up and saw Sarah Spundah opening a lacy silver web into her Forest of Friendship.

"Welcome to my Forest of Friendship," Sarah said sweetly. "I have been expecting you. Your father considers me his royal guardian of the Forest of Friendship because I spin and weave a web of life that connects the lives of all the living creatures in the forest. I also protect the Forest of Friendship so all the people of the kingdom can enjoy its beauty. Princess Shayna, I will be your personal guide on this part of your Vision Quest."

"Sarah Spundah, I feel so safe and secure with you as our guide," the princess replied.

As they walked, Sarah introduced Princess Shayna and White Falcon to all the friendly creatures they met along the path. Sarah told the princess and the white falcon about all the trees, plants, and flowers that grew in the Forest of Friendship, and about their purpose in the web of life.

As they walked farther into the Forest of Friendship, Princess Shayna said enthusiastically, "Sarah Spundah, I am so excited about everything I am learning from you and my new friends."

"Princess Shayna, I am honored and happy that you are enjoying yourself, but I need to rest, for I am a very ancient arachnid," Sarah said.

With her continued enthusiasm, Princess Shayna said. "But, Sarah Spundah, I am so excited to continue."

"Princess Shayna, my legs are becoming very fatigued," Sarah Spundah said. "I could guide you from a pocket close to your heart."

Princess Shayna put Sarah Spundah in the new heart-shaped pocket that magically appeared close to her heart and continued on her Vision Quest through the forest.

"Now I must take a nap, but you must promise to be very careful where you walk. The Forest of Friendship is so new and exciting to you. You could become disoriented and venture down a path that would lead you into the Forest of Fear! Not even the creatures of the Forest of Friendship know exactly where the Forest of Fear is!" Sarah warned.

Princess Shayna promised, "I will be very careful, sweet Sarah."

Then Sarah spun a silken blanket around herself and fell into a sweet slumber inside Princess Shayna's pocket.

You will find reflections about this chapter on page 110 of the Gift Giver's Guide.

Treacherous Trio

Princess Shayna and White Falcon walked deeper into the Forest of Friendship. Suddenly, Princess Shayna stopped and listened. She thought she heard a conversation, but it did not sound like the creatures of the forest. It sounded like two men talking. She followed the voices and came upon two woodsmen who were sitting around a blazing campfire and speaking with the largest raven she had ever seen.

When the raven saw Princess Shayna, it took flight, but not before it circled over the princess, causing a chill to run through her entire body! The princess became frightened and was about to run away when the two woodsmen said, "Do not be afraid, Princess Shayna."

White Falcon warned Princess Shayna, "Do not speak to the two strangers." But she could hardly hear him. When raven Meevillain had circled over the princess, she had used her evil magic to cast a spell of silence upon Princess Shayna.

"What did you say, White Falcon?" she whispered. The Princess could not hear her beloved and devoted companion when he spoke a warning to her.

Princess Shayna cautiously approached the woodsmen. In unison they asked her, "What are you doing all alone in the Forest of Friendship, Princess Shayna?" She trustingly told the woodsmen all about her Vision Quest. She did not know they were really the greedy and treacherous trolls, Mennis and Meene.

The two woodsmen noticed Sarah Spundah sleeping in Princess Shayna's pocket. Meevillain had told them of Sarah's wisdom. "Shhhh, speak quietly so as not to awaken the ancient arachnid," they advised Princess Shayna.

Mennis and Meene then told Princess Shayna, "You can trust us because we have been the royal woodsmen of the forest for many, many years." They assured her that they knew the forest better than anyone. "We can give you the directions to help you on your Vision Quest."

Unsuccessfully, White Falcon tried again to tell the princess not to believe the woodsmen. But Meevillain's magic was growing stronger and stronger. Princess Shayna was unable to hear him.

"I never heard my father speak of you," Princess Shayna told Mennis and Meene.

"Of course not," they told her, "we were appointed by your grandfather many, many years before your father was born." Mennis and Meene continued their deception, "Princess Shayna, in which direction do you want to go?" they asked.

The princess looked at her intuition compass and saw that the silver needle was whirling in a circle and would not stop. Trusting that Mennis and Meene could help her, Princess Shayna said, "My compass is not working properly, but I know that the first stop on my Vision Quest is the Village of the Yellow Sunflowers in the northern part of the kingdom."

Mennis and Meene told her, "Listen carefully, and we will give you expert directions and draw a map for you."

Thinking Mennis and Meene were very kind and helpful, Princess Shayna listened carefully while they gave her directions and drew an erroneous map of the forest. When they were finished, Mennis and Meene said, "Good-bye and good fortune, Princess Shayna."

White Falcon became quite agitated and flapped his powerful wings to warn Princess Shayna not to follow the woodmen's deceitful directions, but the princess thought that he was just excited to continue on their journey.

The unsuspecting princess left the campsite feeling confident and enthusiastic about the remainder of her Vision Quest. Meene and Mennis were quite pleased with how well they had gained Princess Shayna's trust and deceived her. Then they started to quarrel about who would get the princess's precious gifts that she was carrying in her magical pinafore and how they would cook the white falcon for their celebration feast.

While Mennis and Meene argued, Princess Shayna followed their directions that led her into Meevillain's Forest of Fear! And, just as Meevillain had planned, she was getting nowhere fast! Princess Shayna walked deeper and deeper into the Forest of Fear. Suddenly, she felt a chilling wind and a strange sense of foreboding. Meevillain's Forest of Fear began to surround her, and it was becoming darker and darker.

"Every single tree, plant, and flower is dead. White Falcon, Sarah Spundah and I are the only living creatures in this part of the forest. The serenely flowing streams have dried up. The tree trunks are twisted and contorted. The paths are crooked! They go circles and have led me nowhere! They are all dead ends!" the princess exclaimed.

Princess Shayna quickly took out her intuition compass to give herself direction. The needle was still spinning in all directions, which made her very upset and uncomfortable. To calm herself, she took out her kaleidoscope that was always bright and sparkling. She looked into it and saw only darkness. Then she said to herself, "If I light the candles Mimi and Poppy gave me, they will surely illuminate this path of darkness and give me a renewed sense of peacefulness." She circled her hands over the candles three times, just as her grandmother had instructed her, but the candles did not illuminate!

"White Falcon, now I see the light of truth!" Princess Shayna said. She realized that the woodsmen had deceived her. She had put her trust in them. They had not been truthful; they had led her into the Forest of Fear!

White Falcon sat on Princess Shayna's shoulder in silence. He had tried to warn her, but she could not hear him! "I am so frightened. Something is terribly wrong if I can no longer hear you," Princess Shayna said.

An ominous feeling washed over Princess Shayna. *"This must be the feeling of fear—a feeling that I have never known. I am lost in the Forest of Fear,"* she cried. She looked into White Falcon's inquisitive tourmaline eyes for an answer, but there was none. Her beloved and devoted companion remained silent.

As Princess Shayna bravely tried to find her way out of the Forest of Fear, Meevillain's mysterious sleeping mist slowly began to fall and make the princess very tired. She struggled not to fall asleep on the path before she could find her way out of the Forest of Fear.

Exhausted and frustrated from going in circles, Princess Shayna decided to sit down and rest against a large moss-covered rock in the path. The forest was completely dark. She could not see the moon or any stars to guide her out of the Forest of Fear. She said weakly, "It will be best to rest for the night and then start anew in the morning when it will not be so dark and shadowed. Now I must eat and take my silver apricot potion."

Princess Shayna prepared to string an add-a-pearl on the golden necklace. She knew she must keep track of the days of her Vision Quest as she had promised. She knew she must dispense the three drops of silver apricot potion on her finger, as she had promised Sigmund, but she was so tired.

She could not hear White Falcon's protective warning to take care of herself, and a great feeling of disappointment and despair came over her. Princess Shayna fell asleep thinking about the two evil woodsmen. If only she had been more alert, they would not have deceived her.

"If only she could have heard my warning," White Falcon sighed. "If only she had not been so tired, she might have gone a few more steps." Then the princess would have gone around the large moss-covered rock and seen the lush green path that led out of the Meevillain's Forest of Fear and into the Forest of Friendship.

At the same moment that Princess Shayna fell into her deep and dangerous slumber, Sarah Spundah awakened. Sarah realized that the princess would become very ill and freeze to death on the cold, damp floor of the Forest of Fear. "To protect

the princess, I will spin a silken web around her while she sleeps," Sarah Spundah said to White Falcon.

White Falcon replied bravely, "I will fly into the Forest of Friendship and get help from the forest creatures, then I will perch myself on a low-hanging limb of this dead pine tree to watch over and protect the princess until morning. I hope the new day will break Meevillain's evil magic so the princess will be able to hear me again. Then we can continue on her Vision Quest and take the true path out of the Forest of Fear and into the Forest of Friendship."

But before White Falcon could fly off to get help, Meevillain's mysterious sleeping mist made him too weak and tired to fly. Just as she finished spinning her protective silken spider web around Princess Shayna, Sarah Spundah also began to feel very sleepy. She could hardly crawl upon the limb to rest next to White Falcon.

While Princess Shayna, Sarah Spundah, and White Falcon were in a deep and dangerous slumber, Mennis and Meene slithered down the path toward the trusting trio. Raven Meevillain quietly circled overhead to delight in the success of her mysterious sleeping mist. While Meevillain hovered above, Mennis and Meene sneaked up behind the sleeping White Falcon and Sarah Spundah and threw a tightly woven sack over them. Their sinister scheme was to capture White Falcon and Sarah Spundah, and to leave Princess Shayna in the middle of the Forest of Fear to die. Meevillain said, "I have promised to reward Mennis and Meene with all of Princess Shayna's precious gifts after she dies, alone, sick, starved, and frightened in my Forest of Fear."

Mennis and Meene secured the sack with White Falcon and Sarah Spundah inside and took them back to their campsite, deep in the Forest of Fear. Mennis and Meene placed the sack on the ground next to the campfire and began to celebrate. They became so drunk with power that they fell into a senseless stupor. They had forgotten Meevillain's wicked warning, "Do not put the sack too close to the fire. The warmth of the campfire will cause my mysterious sleeping mist to evaporate."

Sarah Spundah and White Falcon slept for three days until, slowly, they were awakened by the warmth of the campfire and the dreadful duo's ranting about their deceitful deeds and Meevillain's evil secret spells. Sarah Spundah and White Falcon listened cautiously until the rhythm of Mennis's and Meene's breathing indicated they were in their drunken stupor again. Cautiously, Sarah squeezed her little silver body out through the threads of the sack. "White Falcon," she instructed, "use your strong beak and your powerful talons to tear open this sack!"

White Falcon tore open the sack and set himself free. Sarah then spun a strong silken web around Mennis and Meene while they slept. White Falcon said, "Sarah, attach your web to the stump of this dead elder tree. We must hurry to find Princess Shayna!"

"I am still drowsy from Meevillain's mysterious sleeping mist," Sarah said sleepily.

White Falcon replied, "I am wide awake. I will fly us out of the Forest of Fear. We must find Princess Shayna before Mennis and Meene wake up and tell Meevillain that we have escaped."

"What a splendid idea," Sarah agreed. She steadily climbed up White Falcon's strong leg, over his powerful wing and onto his majestic white head. "What a vista!" Sarah exclaimed. "I can see everything from up here. I will direct your flight to save Princess Shayna. Do not worry, White Falcon. I know every inch of the forest. Before Meevillain transformed it into her Forest of Fear, I spun my silver silken threads over the many moss-covered paths and gracefully arched canopies of trees to connect all the creatures that inhabit and protect the Forest of Friendship." Sarah Spundah also comforted White Falcon with the promise that her forest friends would have sensed Princess Shayna's predicament and would have proteced her while she slept.

Sarah Spundah was right. While Princess Shayna was fast asleep, Sarah's forest friends did stand watch over the slumbering princess. Their instincts told them she was in great danger and needed their protection. They gathered sweet-smelling moss and branches of lavender to keep her warm, help her sleep peacefully and restore her energy. They were willing to risk their lives and venture into the Forest of Fear to protect the princess, for they too felt the spirit of her Invisible Visible Gift.

As Sarah Spundah and White Falcon flew closer to where Princess Shayna was sleeping, the wind started to sing their approach, and the tree twigs and branches began to tumble to the ground causing all the forest creatures to look up above the Forest of Fear.

"Look up at that wondrous sight," all the forest creatures shouted to one another. "It's Princess Shayna's White Falcon with a small silver crown on his head." The birds in the dead trees took flight to get a closer look at the glorious vision.

Sarah Spundah whispered to White Falcon, "Slow down your powerful wings and let the birds catch up with us, for they surely have brought news about Princess Shayna." As the birds approached White Falcon, they realized it was not a crown on his head, but Sarah Spundah! They guided White Falcon and Sarah down through the twisted dead trees of the Forest of Fear, and directed them to where Princess Shayna lay in a deep, dangerous slumber.

White Falcon was so happy to see Princess Shayna, he extended his wings and flapped them with excitement. The breeze from his powerful wings blew away Meevillain's spell of silence and mysterious sleeping mist, which was clinging to the ground. Aroused by Sarah Spundah's sweet whispers of encouragement, Princess Shayna awakened to the joyful sight of White Falcon with Sarah Spundah crowning his majestic head.

"Princess Shayna, our forest friends said they stood watch over you for three days. You must immediately dispense three drops of your silver apricot potion and eat a little cinnamon cake!" White Falcon said anxiously.

"I can hear you, White Falcon!" Princess Shayna exclaimed. "Meevillain's evil spell of silence has been broken." Princess Shayna quickly dispensed her apricot potion and ate a little cinnamon cake. In a few moments, she was feeling much better.

"There is no time to waste. We must leave this dreadful Forest of Fear," White Falcon instructed.

"Yes, we must hurry and continue our journey safely through the Forest of Friendship," Princess Shayna said as she perched White Falcon on her shoulder.

Sarah Spundah had regained her strength and said, "Follow me. I will spin a silver silken spider web to the Forest of Friendship. It is just beyond this large moss-covered rock."

As the princess followed Sarah, she thanked all the creatures along the path who protected her while she slept. Princess Shayna no longer felt tired and anxious from Meevillain's evil spells, but exhilarated and enthusiastic because of the loving care from her new forest friends.

As they walked toward the edge of the Forest of Friendship, White Falcon told Princess Shayna everything he had learned while she was asleep. Princess Shayna told White Falcon, "I will not let Meevillain and her evil secret spells daunt my commitment to my Vision Quest!"

"That reminds me," said the Princess. "I must keep my promise to Poppy and add three pearls to my necklace. I was just too tired from Meevillain's mysterious sleeping mist to do it. I know it is dangerous to stop, even for a moment, but I must keep my agreement and make sure I return home by the second day of the second month of the new year."

Meanwhile, enraged by Princess Shayna's escape and Mennis and Meene's failure to carry out her orders, Meevillain transformed herself back into her human form and cast a metamorphosing magic spell upon Mennis and Meene. "You will no longer be the false woodsmen of the Forest of Friendship. Instead of changing you back into greedy, treacherous trolls, I will transform you into two worthless worms!"

Meevillain did not give them time to explain themselves. And, as she whirled herself into her raven form, Mennis and Meene became two worthless worms. "Crawl back under the large moss-covered rock from which you came," she commanded. Obediently, the two worthless worms slithered back under the large rock into a pool of slime, never to be seen again.

Raven Meevillain vowed, "I will follow Princess Shayna on the rest of her journey. I will keep her from completing her Vision Quest, never to triumphantly return home to her parents and loved ones!"

With Sarah Spundah's skillful weaving, Princess Shayna and White Falcon quickly arrived at the edge of the Forest of Friendship. Sarah Spundah wished the princess good luck on the rest of her Vision Quest. "I will look forward to your return after you have visited all four villages in the kingdom," Sarah said sweetly. Then Sarah Spundah and her forest friends bid farewell to Princess Shayna and their fearless feathered friend, White Falcon.

Princess Shayna looked across the blooming fields of splendid wild flowers. There she could see the Village of the Yellow Sunflowers.

"White Falcon, I am so excited to see where my mother lived before she became queen," Princess Shayna said.

White Falcon immediately jumped off Princess Shayna's shoulder, extended his powerful wings, and flapped them with excitement. The gentle breeze from his wings caressed her face and made her feel safe and loved once again. Then White Falcon soared gracefully above the princess and guided her toward the Village of the Yellow Sunflowers.

You will find reflections about this chapter on page 111 of the Gift Giver's Guide.

Village of the Yellow Sunflowers

The people of the Village of the Yellow Sunflowers were going about their lives in a very responsible manner when suddenly they heard the wind singing an unusual song—not like the song the wind always sings when the leaves dance, but a different kind of song that could only be made by the wings of the majestic white falcon. They all stood in wonderment as the white falcon soared over the village and then back toward the Forest of Friendship as if he were trying to tell them something.

Then the villagers noticed a figure walking toward their village as if the person were following the path of the white falcon's flight. The villagers began to assemble in an orderly fashion along the yellow stone wall that squarely surrounded their village. A great feeling of hospitality spread among the villagers as they courteously waited for the visitor to arrive.

While the white falcon gracefully circled over the village, the villagers recognized the visitor. "It is Princess Shayna," they said to one another.

Traditional speeches of welcome were made, and all shapes, sizes, and shades of yellow sunflowers were presented to the princess as a gesture of welcome. The princess was overwhelmed by the villagers' thoughtfulness. "Thank you for your most gracious welcome," she said. "Your village is the first visit of my Vision Quest. I will be staying in each village of the kingdom to learn all the lessons I need to know to prove that I am capable and worthy to one day guide and care for the kingdom as your queen. I want to share my Invisible Visible Gift with all of you because I believe it will enable all the villages to work harmoniously together again. And I am confident that you will teach me to recognize and respect your unique perspectives and way of life in the Village of the Yellow Sunflowers."

"Princess Shayna, I have meticulously prepared a special guest chamber in my home, where you and White Falcon can rest," the village elder said as she escorted them to her home.

"I noticed that the villagers' thoughtful welcome seemed to light up the ominous cloud that shadows the kingdom," White Falcon told the princess as they arrived at the village elder's home.

After Princess Shayna and White Falcon rested, drank some fresh sunflower tea and munched on a bowl of roasted sunflower seeds, they joined the village elder in her formal yellow sunflower garden.

"Princess Shayna, while you were resting, I prepared a perfect plan for your visit. Precisely at three o'clock this afternoon, we will begin your tour of our village," the village elder explained. "Our excursion will help you feel comfortable in our village. You will learn your way around very quickly because all the streets are laid out in a precise grid of perfect squares."

When Princess Shayna and White Falcon arrived in the exact center of the Village of the Yellow Sunflowers, they were greeted by a life-sized, perfectly proportioned sculpture of her grandparents and her mother, as a child. The village elder said, "This sculpture was forged as a symbol of respect and admiration for your family. It represents the roots of our community and the foundation our family values have been built upon."

"Now, I think you need some time to explore our village on your own," the village elder said to Princess Shayna. "Everyone is eager to have you learn more about our village. It will be an honor to care for you, and I know you will enjoy your visit with us."

The princess and the white falcon did enjoy their visit in the Village of the Yellow Sunflowers. They made many friends and observed many significant characteristics about the villagers and their community.

"I am very impressed with the exactness of this village. For example, on each home and shop there are the same yellow window flower boxes, shades of yellow weather shutters, and four-sided yellow door knockers," Princess Shayna told White Falcon. "I feel very much at home in this village. It has the same sense of stability that I am accustomed to in my home. I value the villagers' custom to honor and personally care for us as their guests. I feel very safe and happy in this village, just as I do at home."

Promptly at five o'clock every evening, according to the villagers' plan, Princess Shayna and White Falcon enjoyed dinner with a different family. One night after dinner, she told White Falcon, "Each family has been so generous, gracious, and hospitable. Everything is perfect—the food, the conversation, and the accommodations. The villagers have thought of every conceivable detail to make us feel comfortable."

White Falcon said, "Princess Shayna, I enjoy watching how the family members respond to one another. Husbands and wives take their marriage commitments very seriously and work diligently at building an orderly life together. Family members know they can trust and depend on one another. They show their love for one another with practical gifts and sensible deeds."

The princess loved wearing her traditional village uniform like the other girls. They all wore perfectly pressed yellow pinafores similar to the yellow aprons the women wore over their dresses. All the men and boys wore traditionally designed yellow vests and yellow belts with their clothing. The pinafores, aprons, vests, and belts were woven and sewn from many different shades and textures of yellow fabric and leather. They all had pockets that were designed and placed strategically on each garment according to the villager's age or responsibility.

Princess Shayna told White Falcon, "I have noticed that the parents raise their children with appropriate rules and the idea of doing things *the right way*. As small children, they are taught that being responsible is a priority! The adults know that they are accountable for teaching each child proper behavior. There is a great feeling of stability and security in the Village of the Yellow Sunflowers."

Princess Shayna loved going to school with the other youngsters of the village. Many of them had come to play and study with her in the royal castle, and they enjoyed renewing their friendships.

The perfectly square yellow stone school building was well organized for every type of learning the children would need to become successful villagers. The school motto, *Plan Ahead,* hung over each classroom doorway. All the classes displayed the school rules so the children knew which behavior was right and which was wrong. There was never any question about how to be a model student—the children liked following the rules and the structured schedule for their classes. They knew what to expect and what was expected of them.

White Falcon loved exploring the many different shops in the village with the princess. "Look at the sensibly carved signs describing the craft or trade inside each shop," he said.

As they got to know each shopkeeper and merchant, the princess praised the villagers' dedication to their work. "The villagers are proud to be of service to one another," she said. "I appreciate their strong sense of loyalty."

The oldest and busiest building in the village was the village hall. It was built out of yellow stone and was perfectly square. Princess Shayna loved reading all about the community in the village archives, where the village history was stored for safekeeping. As the princess learned more about the people who had lived in the village, she became aware of how proud they were of their past and present accomplishments. She also learned to respect their need to preserve their heritage, customs, and traditions for their well-being.

One night, after a village meeting, Princess Shayna and White Falcon discussed how the villagers always controlled their emotions and took all aspects of their life very seriously. Princess Shayna said, "The villagers do not have time for frivolity. They are very traditional in their thinking and do not easily adjust to changes in their lives."

"Yes, they also get very upset if anything is disorganized. When their plans do not go according to their expectations, they become anxious and worry about their future," White Falcon answered.

Princess Shayna enjoyed complimenting the villagers on how well they handled their daily tasks. The princess noticed that the longer she and the white falcon stayed in the village, the stronger the villagers' feelings of self-confidence and contentment grew. Their way of life seemed to become more like the stories her parents and grandparents had told her about life before the ominous cloud began to shadow the kingdom.

Princess Shayna and White Falcon knew that their visit in the Village of the Yellow Sunflowers was coming to a close. Each night before the princess went to bed, she kept her promise to Poppy. She carefully opened her beautiful amethyst-colored velvet bag and added a pearl to her golden necklace.

Princess Shayna asked the village elder to call a village meeting so that she could thank all the villagers for their hospitality. At the village meeting, she told the villagers, "I am very grateful for the important lessons you have taught me. I have learned to understand and value your many gifts, and I believe your most praiseworthy gifts are your dependability and your capacity for organizing your lives. Now, I must go on to the Village of the Blue Forget-Me-Nots. But before I leave, you must choose a village emissary, who upon my return to your village, will accompany me on my journey home. Your village emissary must verify to the royal advisors that I have learned to understand and value the true meaning of loyalty, responsibility, preparation, and commitment. Your village emissary must also confirm that I have learned the unique lessons from your village that I will need to guide and care for the kingdom and become your future queen."

The villagers were sad that the princess had to leave their village so soon, but felt honored to know that one of them would accompany Princess Shayna and White Falcon home.

The village elder said, "We should select Citrine for such a responsible assignment, for Citrine possesses all the finest qualities of our village."

"We are very proud of her accomplishments, and we value her ability to be respectful, accountable, and thorough," added another villager.

"Yes, Citrine is the perfect person, for she is most trustworthy! She will honestly verify that you have learned everything you need to know from our village to help you become our queen," said another villager.

"Hooray, we have chosen Citrine!" the remaining villagers replied in unison.

Princess Shayna told Citrine. "I will return to your village after I have visited the other three villages on my Vision Quest. Then all four emissaries will accompany White Falcon and me on our journey home to complete my Vision Quest."

Then Citrine spoke, "Princess Shayna, I am honored to have been chosen as my village's emissary. I know we all are sad to see you and White Falcon leave, for we have loved taking care of you and teaching you all about our village. But we understand that you must visit the other villages and share your Invisible Visible Gift with them."

Princess Shayna explained, "I will tell the people of the other villages how you have shared your most praiseworthy gifts with me. I have learned many valuable lessons that will prove that I am capable and worthy to someday guide and care for the kingdom as your queen. I am confident that my Invisible Visible Gift and the knowledge of your gifts will help all the villages live and work in harmony together again!"

The villagers planned a traditional farewell celebration in the village hall for Princess Shayna and White Falcon. "Princess Shayna, as a remembrance of your visit and your commitment to our village, we present you with this yellow sunflower key. It represents the key to our hearts and our village. It is a token of our appreciation for your understanding and respect for our perspectives and lifestyle. It is a gift of gratefulness for accepting us for who we are and what we value. You have shared your Invisible Visible Gift with us and enhanced all the villagers' self-esteem," Citrine said proudly.

"Thank you for your generous gift of acceptance into your community," Princess Shayna said gratefully.

The next day Princess Shayna bid a proper farewell to the villagers. With White Falcon perched on her shoulder and a carefully prepared basket of food for her journey, she approached the sturdy yellow gate that opened to the path that led to the Village of the Blue Forget-Me-Nots. Princess Shayna took the magnificent yellow sunflower key and unlocked the gate. But the gate would not open, for it had not been used since the yellow stone wall had been built around the village when Meevillain's Cloud of Chaos had appeared. Princess Shayna tried with all her strength to open the gate, but it would not budge. Then, with the villagers' help, the gate slowly began to swing open. It revealed a path that once had followed the serenely flowing stream, but now was overgrown and choked with weeds.

Princess Shayna could see that the path would be difficult to travel, but knew the effort would be worthwhile, for she always had her goal in sight. As the villagers watched Princess Shayna leave the shelter of their village, they rejoiced in her enthusiasm for her journey, for they had learned that was how she always approached life!

The villagers were feeling so good and confident about themselves that they called to the Princess, "Wait, we want to help you!" And they began to carefully tear down their yellow stone wall.

"We will use the stones to pave a new path to the Village of the Blue Forget-Me-Nots. We no longer need a wall to separate us from the other villages. We have learned to value our gifts because of your Invisible Visible Gift, and we wish to share them with the other villages," the villagers exclaimed.

"Look up," Citrine said. The villagers who were paving the path looked to the sky. "Our new path lights up the ominous cloud that has shadowed the brightness of the kingdom," she said.

But only Citrine detected the mysterious raven concealing itself behind the ominous cloud. Citrine had also observed the bird secretly circling over the village every day since Princess Shayna had arrived. Every time Citrine saw the raven, she felt a chill go through her entire body. And, although she was worried, she told no one, for she did not want to worry anyone else.

"I will guide you and the villagers to the Village of the Blue Forget-Me-Nots," White Falcon told Princess Shayna, as he excitedly jumped off her shoulder. He extended his powerful wings and soared gracefully above the princess and the villagers as they carefully paved the new path.

Citrine said to Princess Shayna, "The villagers are very proud of the bright new path they are building to connect the Village of the Yellow Sunflowers to the Village of the Blue Forget-Me-Nots!"

You will find reflections about this chapter
on page 112 of the Gift Giver's Guide.

Village of the Blue Forget-Me-Nots

The people of the Village of the Blue Forget-Me-Nots were going about their lives in a very harmonious manner when suddenly they heard the wind singing an unusual song—not like the song the wind sings when the leaves dance, but a different kind of song that could only be made by the wings of the majestic white falcon. They all stood in wonderment as the white falcon soared over the village and then back down the path that led from the Village of the Yellow Sunflowers. It looked as if he were trying to tell them something.

Then the villagers noticed a figure walking toward their village, as if it were following the path of the white falcon's flight. They also saw a bright yellow stone path that they had never seen before. A great feeling of excitement spread among the villagers as they eagerly waited for the visitor to arrive.

While the white falcon gracefully circled over the village, the villagers recognized the visitor. "It is Princess Shayna," they said to one another. "Who are the other people with her? They look so different. They are actually paving a perfect bright yellow stone path right up to our blue stone wall that creatively circles our Village of Blue Forget-Me-Nots," the villagers said dubiously.

The people from the Village of the Yellow Sunflowers stayed just outside the blue stone wall of the Village of the Blue Forget-Me-Nots. Princess Shayna could feel their discomfort and concern for her. Gently, she told them, "Please do not to worry about me. I am sure the people from the Village of the Blue Forget-Me-Nots will be respectful of me. Remember, the blue forget-me-not villagers have not learned about the Invisible Visible Gift as you have. It will take them time to learn how to share their gifts."

Princess Shayna waved farewell to the yellow sunflower villagers and entered the Village of the Blue Forget-Me-Nots, where she was welcomed with friendly speeches and presented with all shapes, sizes, and shades of blue forget-me-nots.

The
princess was
overwhelmed by the villagers'
thoughtfulness. "Thank you for your loving welcome," she told the villagers.
"Your village is the second visit of my Vision Quest. I will be staying in each village
of the kingdom to learn all the lessons I need to know to prove that I am capable
and worthy to one day guide and care for the kingdom as your queen. I want to
share my Invisible Visible Gift with all of you because I believe it will enable all the
villages to work harmoniously together again. And I am confident that you will teach
me to recognize and respect your unique perspectives and way of life in the Village
of the Blue-Forget-Me-Nots."

"Princess Shayna, I have joyfully prepared a special guest chamber in my home,
where you and White Falcon can rest," the village elder said as she escorted them to
her home.

"I noticed that the villagers' loving welcome seemed to light up the ominous
cloud that shadows the kingdom," White Falcon told the princess as they arrived at
the village elder's home.

56

After Princess Shayna and White Falcon rested, drank some fresh blueberry tea and munched on a bowl of roasted blueberries, they joined the village elder in her informal blue forget-me-not garden.

"Princess Shayna, while you were resting, I thought about many sites in our community that I would like to share with you. We can talk about them as we begin your tour of our village," village elder explained. "Our excursion will help you feel comfortable in our village. You will learn your way around very quickly because all the streets in our village are circular and connect to one another.

When Princess Shayna and the village elder arrived in the approximate center of the village, there was a life-sized sculpture of the village's greatest artists. The village elder said, "These are the writers, actors, painters, sculptors, musicians, singers, poets, and dancers who have brought an appreciation for the arts and their talents to our community."

"Now, I think you need some time to explore our village on your own," the village elder said to Princess Shayna. "We are eager to have you learn more about our village. It will be our pleasure to help you in any way we can, and I know you will be very happy while you visit with us."

The princess and the white falcon did enjoy their visit in the Village of the Blue Forget-Me-Nots. While they lived in the village, they made many friends and noticed many meaningful characteristics about the villagers and their community.

"I am impressed with the uniqueness of the village. Look at each home and shop. There are different sizes of blue window flower boxes, different shades of blue weather shutters, and round blue doorbells," Princess Shayna told White Falcon. "I feel very comfortable in this village. It reminds me of my dear friends, Lord John and Lady Michelle. My intuition tells me that the villagers value integrity and consideration for people's feelings. I feel safe and happy in this village, just as I do at home."

Between five and six o'clock every evening, Princess Shayna and White Falcon enjoyed dinner with a different family. One night after dinner, she told White Falcon,

"Family members are very secure in their relationships with one another. I delight in watching how they nurture one another. Husbands and wives are very affectionate and thoughtful of one another and work at building a peaceful life together. The villagers often give family members sentimental gifts and gestures of affection. The longer we visit in this village, the more I learn to appreciate the villagers' imagination and flexibility."

White Falcon said, "I greatly appreciate everyone's ability to be compassionate and understanding. The villagers give me a genuine feeling of warmth and friendliness. Everyone has been very considerate."

Princess Shayna loved wearing her creatively designed village clothing. None of the villagers' outfits were the same. Everyone wore something unique to themselves, but they all wore a blue heart somewhere on their clothing. It appeared on their sleeves, their hats, the hems of their skirts, the pockets of their pants, or the buttons on their clothes. Everyone's outfit was artistic and original, no matter what the person's age or responsibility in the village.

Princess Shayna told White Falcon, "I have noticed that parents raise their children with family values and the idea of cooperation! Every adult feels accountable for teaching each child a sense of community. As small children, they are taught that taking care of one another is the family priority! There is a great feeling of kinship in the Village of the Blue Forget-Me-Nots."

Princess Shayna loved going to school with the other youngsters of the village. Many of them had come to play and study with her in the royal castle, and they enjoyed renewing their friendships with her.

The attractive blue stone school building was constructed for every type of learning to help the children become caring and creative villagers. The school motto, *Help Others,* was artistically painted over the entrance to each classroom. Getting to

know each other was an important part of the children's education. Pictures of all the children and their favorite extracurricular activities were displayed in every classroom. The children loved school. They were encouraged to ask questions and to use their imaginations both inside and outside the classroom!

White Falcon loved visiting the different shops or merchant carts in the village with the princess. "Look at the decoratively carved signs showing the talents of each merchant," he said.

As they got to know each shopkeeper and merchant, the princess praised the villagers' attitude to do an exemplary job. "They are very cooperative with one another," she said. "I appreciate their willingness to listen to one another."

The oldest and busiest building in the village was the community arts center. It was constructed with variegated blue stones and had many rooms, where the villagers could attend their celebrations and social events together. The center gave the villagers a strong sense of self-expression and authenticity in their life.

One night after a village meeting, Princess Shayna and White Falcon discussed how the villagers did not always control their emotions, that they would get upset if people were not getting along with one another. Princess Shayna said, "When the community is not working together, the villagers become depressed and sensitive about their lives."

"They are very intuitive and make decisions based on how they feel at the time. They are very passionate, and their feelings get hurt easily," White Falcon answered.

The princess was delighted when she complimented the villagers on how well they handled their daily tasks. She noticed that the longer she and the white falcon stayed in the village, the stronger the villagers' feelings of self-confidence and contentment grew. Their way of life seemed to become more like the stories her parents and grandparents had told her about life before the ominous cloud began to shadow the kingdom.

Princess Shayna and White Falcon knew that their visit in the Village of the Blue Forget-Me-Nots was nearing its end. Each night before going to bed, the princess kept her promise to Poppy. She carefully opened her amethyst-colored velvet bag and added a pearl to her golden necklace.

Princess Shayna asked the village elder to call a village meeting so that she could thank the villagers for their hospitality. At the meeting, she told the villagers, "I am grateful for the important lessons you have taught me. I have learned to understand and value your many gifts, and I believe your most praiseworthy gifts are your helpfulness and your ability to passionately inspire others. Now, I must go on to the Village of the Orange Tiger Lilies. But before I leave, you must choose a village emissary who, upon my return to your village, will accompany me on my journey home. Your village emissary must verify to the royal advisors that I have learned to understand and value the true meaning of helpfulness, friendship, compassion, truthfulness, and respect for the land's natural wonders. Your village emissary must also confirm that I have learned the unique lessons from your village that I will need to guide and care for the kingdom and become your future queen."

The villagers were very sad that the princess had to leave their village so soon, but felt honored to know that one of them would accompany Princess Shayna and White Falcon home.

The village elder said, "We should select Spinel for such an inspiring assignment, for Spinel possesses all the finest qualities of our village."

"We are proud of her accomplishments, and we value her integrity, consideration, and creative talents," added another villager.

"Spinel is the perfect person, for she is most trustworthy. She will honestly verify that you have learned everything you need to know from our village to help you become our queen," said another villager.

"Hooray, we have chosen Spinel!" the villagers replied in unison.

Princess Shayna told Spinel, "I will return to your village after I have visited the other two villages on my Vision Quest. Then all four emissaries will accompany White Falcon and me on our journey home to complete my Vision Quest."

Then Spinel spoke, "Princess Shayna, I am honored to have been chosen as my village emissary. We all are very sad to see you and White Falcon leave, for we have loved getting to know you better and teaching you all about our village. But we understand that you must visit the other villages and share your Invisible Visible Gift with them also."

Princess Shayna explained, "I will tell the people in the other villagers how you have shared your most praiseworthy gifts with me. I have learned many valuable lessons that will prove that I am capable and worthy to someday guide and care for the kingdom as your queen. I am confident that my Invisible Visible Gift and the knowledge of your gifts will help all the villages live and work in harmony together again!"

The villagers gave a loving farewell celebration in the community art center for Princess Shayna and White Falcon. "Princess Shayna, as a remembrance of your visit and your commitment to our village, we present you with this blue forget-me-not key. It represents the key to our hearts and our village. It is a token of our appreciation for your understanding and respect for our perspectives and lifestyle. It is a gift of gratefulness for accepting us for who we are and what we value. You have shared your Invisible Visible Gift with us and enhanced all the villagers' self-esteem," Spinel said emotionally.

"Thank you for your generous gift of acceptance into your community," Princess Shayna said gratefully.

The next day Princess Shayna bid an emotional farewell to the villagers. With White Falcon perched on her shoulder and a thoughtfully prepared basket of food for her journey, she approached the sturdy blue gate that opened to the path that led to the Village of the Orange Tiger Lilies. Princess Shayna took the magnificent blue forget-me-not key and unlocked the gate. But it did not open, for it had not been used since the blue stone wall had been built around the village. The princess pushed again, but it did not budge. The villagers joined in the effort, and slowly the gate began to open. It revealed a path that once had followed the serenely flowing stream, but now was overgrown and choked with weeds.

Princess Shayna could see that the path would be difficult, but she knew the effort would be worthwhile, for she always had her goal in sight. As the villagers watched Princess Shayna leave the shelter of their village, they rejoiced in her enthusiasm for her journey, for they had learned that was how she always approached life!

Feeling very good and confident about themselves, the villagers called to the Princess, "Wait, we all want to help you!" And they began to tear down their blue stone wall. "We will use the stones to pave a new path to the Village of the Orange Tiger Lilies. We no longer need a wall to separate us from the other villages. We have learned to value our gifts because of your Invisible Visible Gift, and we wish to share them with the other villages," the villagers exclaimed.

"Look up," Spinel said. The villagers who had begun paving the path looked to the sky. "Our new path lights up the ominous cloud that has shadowed the brightness of the kingdom."

But only Spinel detected the mysterious raven concealing itself behind the ominous cloud. She had seen the bird circling over the village every day since the princess had arrived and, each time, she felt a chill go through her entire body. Spinel was frightened but told no one, for she did not want to frighten the other villagers.

"I will help guide you and the villagers toward the village of the Orange Tiger Lilies," White Falcon told Princess Shayna as he excitedly jumped off her shoulder. He extended his powerful wings and glided gracefully above the princess and the happy villagers as they paved the new path.

Spinel turned to the princess and said, "The villagers are very proud of the bright new path they are building to connect the Village of the Blue Forget-Me-Nots to the Village of the Orange Tiger Lilies!"

You will find reflections about this chapter on page 113 of the Gift Giver's Guide.

Village of the Orange Tiger Lilies

The people of the Village of the Orange Tiger Lilies were going about their lives in a very energetic manner, when they suddenly heard the wind singing an unusual song—not like the song the wind sings when the leaves dance, but a different kind of song that could only be made by the wings of the majestic white falcon. They all stood in wonderment as the white falcon soared over the village and then back down the path that led from the Village of the Blue Forget-Me-Nots. It looked as if he were trying to tell them something.

Then the villagers noticed a figure walking toward their village as if it were following the path of the white falcon's flight. They also saw a bright blue stone path that they had never seen before. A great feeling of excitement spread among the villagers as they impatiently waited for the visitor to arrive.

While the white falcon gracefully circled over the village, the villagers recognized the visitor. "It is Princess Shayna," they said to one another. "Who are the other people with her? They look different. They are actually paving a path with a variety of bright blue stones right up to our orange stone wall that freely meanders around our Village of the Orange Tiger Lilies," the villagers said suspiciously.

The people from the Village of the Blue Forget-Me-Nots stayed just outside the orange stone wall of the Village of the Orange Tiger Lilies. Princess Shayna could feel their discomfort and concern for her. Gently, she told them, "Please do not be concerned about me, I am sure the people from the Village of the Orange Tiger Lilies will be considerate of me. Remember, the orange tiger lily villagers have not learned about the Invisible Visible Gift as you have. It will take them time to learn how to share their gifts."

Princess Shayna waved good-bye to the blue forget-me-not villagers and entered the Village of the Orange Tiger Lilies. She was greeted with entertaining speeches of welcome and all shapes, sizes, and shades of orange tiger lilies.

The
princess was
overwhelmed
by the villagers'
enthusiasm. "Thank you for
your most exciting welcome," she told the
villagers. "Your village is the third visit of my Vision Quest. I will be staying in each
village of the kingdom to learn all the lessons I need to know to prove that I am
capable and worthy to one day guide and care for the kingdom as your queen. I
want to share my Invisible Visible Gift with all of you because I believe it will enable
all the villages to work harmoniously together again. And I am confident that you will
teach me to recognize and respect your unique perspectives and way of life in the
Village of the Orange Tiger Lilies."

"Princess Shayna, I will quickly prepare a special guest chamber in my home,
where you and the white falcon can rest," the village elder said as he escorted them
to his home.

"I noticed that the villagers' exciting welcome seemed to light up the ominous
cloud that shadows the kingdom," the white falcon told the princess as they arrived
at the village elder's home.

After Princess Shayna and White Falcon rested, drank some fresh orange spiced
tea, and munched on a bowl of roasted orange peels, they joined the village elder in
his vibrant orange tiger lily garden.

"Princess Shayna, while you were resting, I had so much fun thinking about the activities that I would like to share with you while you live in our community. Let's get started right now! We can talk about what you would like to do as we tour the village," the village elder explained. "Our excursion will help you feel comfortable in our village. You will have fun learning your way because the streets create interesting and varied patterns that go in every direction. Sometimes they connect and sometimes they don't. It will be a game to learn your way around the village."

When the princess and the white falcon reached an area somewhere near the middle of the village, they were quite surprised. There was a tremendous park! Unlike the other villages, there was no large building or life-sized sculpture. Instead, there were villagers of every age engaging in variety of athletic activities. There were large open spaces and special play areas just for young children to explore. Everyone was having such a good time together. The village elder said, "The village park is here for all the villagers to learn to share and appreciate the importance of good sportsmanship and adventure."

"Now, I think you need some time to explore our village on your own," the village elder said to Princess Shayna. "Everyone is eager for you to learn more about our village. It will be lots of fun to show you a good time, and I know you will not be bored while you are here."

The princess and the white falcon did enjoy their visit in the Village of Orange Tiger Lilies. While they lived in the village, they made many friends and noticed many remarkable characteristics about the villagers and their community.

"I am impressed with the freedom of self-expression in the village. Look at each home and shop. There are different sizes of orange window flower boxes, many shades of orange weather shutters, and whimsical orange-shaped door knockers. None of the buildings resemble one another." Princess Shayna told White Falcon. "In this village, I feel like a small child again!"

"I know just how you feel," White Falcon responded. "Remember, this village was actually my first home as a young falcon. When I was very young, everyone remarked that there was something special about me. They said I was a magnificent sight to behold when I soared freely in the sky above the village. I always loved to perform daring feats for the villagers.

"Lady Lillian and Lord Joseph were so proud of me. They nurtured my courage and resourcefulness. They said that I demonstrated an unusual zest for life, as if I possessed a powerful human spirit," he said proudly. "They raised me with the values that enabled me to become your most beloved and devoted companion."

Depending on what the princess was doing or where she was, she enjoyed a fun-loving evening with a different family. The family dinners were always spontaneous—nothing was ever prepared ahead of time. One night after a picnic, she told White Falcon, "The villagers often show family members how much they love them by surprising them with generous gifts and giving lots of affectionate hugs. Husbands and wives are very attentive toward one another and work at building an exciting life together."

"The families do not like a structured lifestyle. They love being spontaneous. If people have differences with each other, they don't get angry. Instead, they eagerly work together toward an agreement. Taking action and doing something about a problem is their method of getting along with one another," White Falcon said.

The princess loved wearing her unconventional village costume and accessories. All the villagers wore comfortable costumes, so they could easily enjoy the activities in the village park. They also carried a variety of orange colored sacks, backpacks, and purses to keep their toys and tools in, depending on their age or responsibility in the village.

Princess Shayna told White Falcon, "I have noticed that the parents raise their children with the courage and confidence to take risks and enjoy the challenges of life. The adults give the children a strong sense of optimism and enthusiasm. As small children, they are taught that experiencing life to the fullest is a priority! There is a sense of enjoying the moment and not worrying about the past or the future in the Village of the Orange Tiger Lilies."

Princess Shayna loved going to school with the other youngsters of the village. Many of them had come to play and study with her in the royal castle, and they enjoyed renewing their friendships.

The charming orange stone school was constructed for every type of hands-on learning the children would need to become skillful and adventurous people. The school did not have set routines or time schedules for their studies, and the children worked at their own level of interest. The students were always encouraged to test their limits and to experience new activities. The teachers encouraged the children to enjoy competition and be spontaneous both in and out of the classroom! The school motto, *Let's Do It!* was vividly painted over each classroom entrance. All the classrooms were different, and many had areas for outside activities.

Let's Do It !

White Falcon loved visiting the different shops, tents, and merchant carts in the village with the princess. "Look at the whimsically carved signs that describe the activity of each merchant," he said.

As they got to know each merchant, the princess praised the villagers' love for working with tools and making amazing toys for the village children, no matter what their age. "I appreciate the shopkeepers' strong sense of camaraderie. They are skillful and clever," she said.

The oldest and busiest building in the Village of the Orange Tiger Lilies was the community park lodge. Built out of orange stone, it had many rooms inside and lots of space outside for the villagers to hold sporting events and theatrical productions. There were so many activities taking place, the villagers never got bored. The community park lodge gave the villagers a strong sense of freedom and variety in their lives.

One night after a village meeting, Princess Shayna and White Falcon discussed how the villagers did not like having anyone control them. Princess Shayna said, "They never like taking directions from other people and love having fun and taking risks! The villagers are very adventurous and welcome changes in their lives. They need variety and dislike anything that is redundant. When the villagers are not able to live their lives the way they want to, they get very upset."

White Falcon observed, "They can be very impulsive, and when the villagers are waiting for decisions to be made, they often become impatient."

Princess Shayna had fun complimenting the villagers on how well they handled their daily tasks. She noticed that the longer she and White Falcon stayed in the village, the stronger the villagers' feelings of self-confidence and contentment grew. Their way of life seemed to become more like the stories her parents and grandparents had told her about life before the ominous cloud began to shadow the kingdom.

Princess Shayna and White Falcon knew that their visit in the Village of the Orange Tiger Lilies was coming to a close. Keeping her promise to Poppy, the princess carefully opened her amethyst-colored bag and added a pearl to her golden necklace each night.

The princess asked the village elder to call a village meeting so that she could thank the villagers for their hospitality. At the village meeting, she told everyone, "I am grateful for the important lessons you have taught me. I have learned to understand and value your many gifts, but I believe your most praiseworthy gifts are your courage and living your lives to their fullest. Now, I must go on to the Village of the Green Healing Herbs. But before I leave, you must choose a village emissary who, upon my return to your village, will accompany me on my journey home. Your village emissary must verify to the royal advisors that I have learned to understand and value the true meaning of courage, resourcefulness, open-mindedness, and the vitality of life. Your village emissary must also confirm that I have learned the unique lessons from your village that I will need to guide and care for the kingdom and become your future queen."

The villagers were sad that the princess had to leave their village so soon, but felt honored to know that one of them would accompany Princess Shayna and White Falcon home.

The village elder said, "We should select Padparadscha for such an exciting assignment, for Padparadscha possesses all the finest qualities of our village."

"We are proud of his accomplishments, and we value his skills to be courageous, think spontaneously, and have fun," added another villager.

"Padparadscha is the perfect person, for he is most trustworthy! He will honestly verify that you have learned everything you need to know from our village to help you become our queen," said another villager.

"Hooray, we have chosen Padparadscha!" the villagers replied in unison.

Princess Shayna told Padparadscha, "I will return to your village after I have visited the last village on my Vision Quest. Then all four emissaries will accompany White Falcon and me on our journey home to complete my Vision Quest."

Then Padparadscha spoke, "Princess Shayna, I am honored to have been chosen as my village emissary. We are very sad to see you and White Falcon leave, for we have loved getting to know you better and teaching you all about our village. But we understand that you must visit the other village and share your Invisible Visible Gift with them also."

Princess Shayna explained, "I will tell the people of the other villages how you have shared your most praiseworthy gifts with me. I have learned many valuable lessons that will prove that I am capable and worthy to someday guide and care for the kingdom as your queen. I am confident that my Invisible Visible Gift and the knowledge of your gifts will help all the villages live and work in harmony together again!"

The villagers had a spontaneous and jubilant farewell celebration in the community park lodge for the princess and the white falcon. "Princess Shayna, as a remembrance of your visit and your commitment to our village, we present you with this orange tiger lily key. It represents the key to our hearts and our village. It is a token of our appreciation for your understanding and respect for our perspectives and lifestyle. It is a gift of gratefulness for accepting us for who we are and what we value. You have shared your Invisible Visible Gift with us and enhanced all the villagers' self-esteem," Padparadscha said proudly.

"Thank you for your generous gift of acceptance into your community," Princess Shayna said gratefully.

The next day Princess Shayna bid an energetic farewell to the villagers. With White Falcon perched on her shoulder and a skillfully prepared basket of food for her journey, she approached the sturdy orange gate that opened to the path that led to the Village of the Green Healing Herbs. Princess Shayna took the magnificent orange tiger lily key and unlocked the gate. But the gate did not open, for it had not been used since the orange stone wall had been built around the village. Princess Shayna tried with all her strength to open the gate, but it would not budge. The villagers joined her, and together they slowly pushed the gate open. It revealed a path that once had followed the serenely flowing stream, but now was overgrown and choked with weeds.

Princess Shayna could see that the path would be as difficult to travel as the previous two paths. But she knew the effort would be worthwhile, for she always had her goal in sight. As the villagers watched Princess Shayna leave the shelter of their village, they rejoiced in her enthusiasm for her journey, for they had learned that was how she always approached life!

The villagers were feeling so good and confident about themselves that they called to the Princess, "Wait, we all want to help you!" Then they began to eagerly tear down their orange stone wall.

"We will use the stones to pave a new path to the Village of the Green Healing Herbs. We no longer need a wall to separate us from the other villages. We have learned to value our gifts because of your Invisible Visible Gift and wish to share them with the other villages," the villagers exclaimed.

"Look up," Padparadscha said. The other villagers stopped paving and eagerly looked to the sky. "Our new path lights up the ominous cloud that has shadowed the brightness of the kingdom."

But only Padparadscha detected the mysterious raven concealing itself behind the ominous cloud. He had also observed the bird secretly circling over the village every day since

Princess Shayna had arrived. Every time Padparadscha saw the raven, he felt a chill go through his entire body. Padparadscha felt very uneasy but told no one, for he did not want to upset anyone else.

"I will guide you and the villagers toward the village of the Green Healing Herbs," White Falcon told Princess Shayna, as he excitedly jumped off her shoulder. He extended his powerful wings and glided gracefully above the princess and the excited villagers as they paved the new path.

Padparadscha told Princess Shayna, "The villagers are very proud of the bright new path they are building to connect the Village of the Orange Tiger Lilies to the Village of the Green Healing Herbs!"

You will find reflections about this chapter
on page 114 of the Gift Giver's Guide.

Village of the Green Healing Herbs

The people of the Village of the Green Healing Herbs were going about their lives in a very intelligent manner when they heard the wind singing an unusual song—not like the song the wind sings when the leaves dance, but a different kind of song that could only be made by the wings of the majestic white falcon. They all stood in wonderment as the white falcon soared over the village and then back down the path that led from the Village of the Orange Tiger Lilies. It looked as if he were trying to tell them something.

Then the villagers noticed a figure walking toward their village as if it were following the path of the white falcon's flight. They also saw a bright orange stone path that they had never seen before. A great feeling of curiosity spread among the villagers as they prudently waited for the visitor to arrive.

While the white falcon gracefully circled over the village, the villagers recognized the visitor. "It is Princess Shayna," they said to one another. "Who are the other people with her? They look different. They are actually paving a bright orange stone path right up to our green stone wall that methodically encompasses our Village of Green Healing Herbs," the villagers said very cautiously.

The people from the Village of the Orange Tiger Lilies stayed just outside the green stone wall of the Village of the Green Healing Herbs. Princess Shayna could feel their discomfort and concern for her. Gently, she told them, "Please do not to worry about me, I am sure the people from the Village of the Green Healing Herbs will be respectful of me. Remember, the green healing herb villagers have not learned about the Invisible Visible Gift as you have. It will take them time to learn how to share their gifts.

Princess Shayna said good-bye to the orange tiger lily villagers. She entered the Village of the Green Healing Herbs, where intelligent speeches of welcome were made, and all shapes, sizes, and shades of green healing herbs were presented to her as a gesture of welcome.

The princess was overwhelmed by the villagers' knowledge. "Thank you for your most logical welcome," she told the villagers. "Your village is the fourth visit of my Vision Quest. I am staying in each village of the kingdom to learn all the lessons I need to know to prove that I am capable and worthy to one day guide and care for the kingdom as your queen. I want to share my Invisible Visible Gift with all of you because I believe it will enable all the villages to work harmoniously together again. And I am confident that you will teach me to recognize and respect your unique perspectives and way of life in the Village of the Green Healing Herbs," the princess added.

"Princess Shayna, I have intelligently prepared a special guest chamber in my home, where you and White Falcon can rest," the village elder said as he escorted them to her home.

"I noticed that the villagers' logical welcome seemed to light up the ominous cloud that shadows the kingdom," White Falcon told the princess as they arrived at the village elder's home.

After Princess Shayna and White Falcon rested, drank some fresh green herbal tea, and munched on a bowl of roasted juniper berries, they joined the village elder in his aesthetic green healing herb garden.

"Princess Shayna, while you were resting, I developed a strategy for your visit," the village elder explained. "Our excursion will help you master the design of our village. You will learn your way around very quickly because there is a precise system to our streets. The streets are arranged like the spokes of a wheel, but the villagers are always working on how to make the system better."

When the princess and the white falcon arrived in the precise center of the village, there was a life-sized sculpture of the village's greatest scholars and inventors who had brought the appreciation for new knowledge and study to the village. The villagers admired their philosophies, nonconformity, and great vision.

"Now, I think you need some time to explore our village on your own," the village elder said to Princess Shayna. "We are impressed that you want to learn more about our village. It will be our privilege to teach you everything you need to know while you visit with us."

The princess and the white falcon did enjoy their visit in the Village of Green Healing Herbs. While they lived in the village, they made many friends and studied the many exceptional characteristics about the villagers and their community.

"I am impressed with the competency of the village. Look at all the homes and shops. They all have architecturally correct green window flower boxes, diverse shades of green weather shutters, and geometrically shaped green door chimes. All the buildings are built to increase efficiency and respect everyone's privacy," Princess Shayna told White Falcon.

Princess Shayna felt very much at home in the Village of the Green Healing Herbs, for the villagers reminded her of her dear friend Lord Markus. She knew the villagers valued education, independence, and fairness as she was accustomed to at home.

Every evening Princess Shayna and White Falcon enjoyed dinner with a different family. Dinner was never at a regular time because the villagers often became so engrossed in their daily tasks that they forgot what time it was. One night after dinner, the princess told White Falcon, "I appreciate the villagers' quiet hospitality and calm attitudes. When I ask a question, the villagers answer with clear and thorough explanations. They are very mindful of us, but they are reserved with displays of their affections. Husbands and wives are not physically attentive to each other, but I am confident they are extremely sensitive to one another privately."

"It isn't easy for green healing herb villagers to show their emotions and love for their families and one another. They do not think with their hearts, but with their heads. They always analyze their responses and behave wisely. In fact, I have observed that they actually are more sensitive than the blue-forget-me-not villagers," White Falcon said.

Princess Shayna loved wearing her practical garments and thinking cap. Each villager's hat, bonnet or hood was made from a different shade and texture of green fabric. Everyone was sensibly attired according to age or responsibility in the village.

Princess Shayna told White Falcon, "I have noticed that all parents raise their children with a great thirst for knowledge and a strong commitment to education. The children are taught that being logical is a priority! Each villager is accountable for teaching every child a sense of justice and insight into their future for life-long study and learning."

The princess loved going to school with the youngsters of the village. Many of them had come to play and study with her in the royal castle, and they enjoyed renewing their friendships.

The accurately proportioned green stone school building was designed for *every type* of intellectual scholarship the children needed to become mentally focused and mature individuals. The school motto, *Be Logical*, was painted over the entrance to each classroom. The classrooms had individual learning alcoves with all the books and tools needed for abstract and concrete thinking. The children worked independently of one another and developed their own learning systems. The students strived for perfection and learned to solve problems for themselves by taking time to research and think about all the possible answers. The teachers encouraged the children's curiosity.

White Falcon loved visiting the different shops in the village with the princess. "Look at the expertly carved signs describing the shopkeepers, who are totally absorbed in their work or invention," he said.

As they got to know the merchants, they realized that the people considered work as play. Princess Shayna praised everyone for their individuality and quality of their workmanship. "The shopkeepers are courteous and fair," she said. "I appreciate their innovative minds."

The oldest and busiest building in the Village of the Green Healing Herbs was the village library. It was built out of green stones that were copiously covered with dark green ivy. The library had many quiet rooms inside and tranquil spaces outside. There the villagers could read, study, and reflect on their strong sense of living by their own standards and maintaining a systematic order in their lives.

One night after a village meeting, Princess Shayna and White Falcon discussed how the villagers liked to be calm, cool, and collected. Princess Shayna said, "They are not patient with individuals who they think are not smart, and they never want to look foolish or stupid. The villagers take themselves very seriously and never like to be laughed at. They also are very analytical thinkers and make changes in their lives only after lengthy research and contemplation."

"The villagers get upset if people are incompetent or repetitious. When they have to deal with incompetence, they become indecisive and withdrawn," White Falcon said.

The princess liked complimenting the villagers about how well they handled their daily tasks. She noticed that the longer she and the white falcon stayed in the village, the stronger the villagers' feelings of self-confidence and contentment grew. Their way of life seemed to become more like the stories her parents and grandparents had told her about life before the ominous cloud began to shadow the kingdom.

Princess Shayna and White Falcon knew that their visit in the Village of the Green Healing Herbs was coming to a close. Each night before the princess went to bed, she kept her promise to Poppy. She carefully opened her amethyst-colored bag and added a pearl to her golden necklace.

Princess Shayna asked the village elder to call a village meeting so that she could thank all the villagers for their hospitality. At the village meeting, she told the villagers, "I am very grateful for the remarkable and important lessons you have taught me. I have learned to understand and value your many gifts, and I believe your most praiseworthy gifts are your innovative minds and your love for knowledge. Now, I must return home. But before I leave, you must choose a village emissary who will accompany me on my journey home. Your village emissary must verify to the royal advisors that I have learned to understand and value the true meaning of logical thinking, individuality, justice, and seeking knowledge. Your village emissary must also confirm that I have learned the unique lessons from your village that I will need to guide and care for the kingdom and become your future queen," Princess Shayna told the villagers.

The villagers were sad that the princess had to leave their village so soon, but felt honored to know that one of them would accompany Princess Shayna and White Falcon home.

The village elder said, "We should select Peridot for such an honorable assignment, for Peridot possesses all the finest qualities of our village."

"We are very proud of his accomplishments, and we value his aptitude to be logical, composed, and keep an accurate record of Princess Shayna's Vision Quest," added another villager.

"Yes, Peridot is the perfect person, for he is most trustworthy! He will honestly verify that you have learned everything you need to know from our village to help you become our queen," said another villager.

"Hooray, we have chosen Peridot!" the villagers replied in unison.

Princess Shayna told Peridot. "You will accompany me to the other three villages to assemble the emissaries for the completion of my Vision Quest. Then you all will accompany me and White Falcon on our journey home."

Then Peridot spoke, "Princess Shayna, I am honored to have been chosen as my village emissary. We are sad to see you and White Falcon leave, for we have loved getting to know you better and teaching you all about our village."

Princess Shayna explained, "I will tell the people of the other villages how you have shared your most praiseworthy gifts with me. I have learned many valuable lessons that will prove that I am capable and worthy to someday guide and care for the kingdom as your queen. I am confident that my Invisible Visible Gift and the knowledge of your gifts will help the villages live and work in harmony together again!"

The villagers planned an innovative farewell celebration in the village library for Princess Shayna and White Falcon. "Princess Shayna, as a remembrance of your visit and your commitment to our village, we present you with this green healing herb key. It represents the key to our hearts and our village. It is a token of our appreciation for your understanding and respect for our perspectives and lifestyle. It is a gift of gratefulness for accepting us for who we are and what we value. You have shared your Invisible Visible Gift with us and enhanced all the villagers' self-esteem," Peridot said proudly.

"Thank you for your generous gift of acceptance into your community," Princess Shayna said gratefully.

The next day Princess Shayna bid a sensible farewell to the villagers. With White Falcon perched on her shoulder and a perfectly prepared basket of food for her journey, she approached the sturdy green gate that opened to the path that led to the Village of the Yellow Sunflowers. Princess Shayna took the magnificent green healing herb key and unlocked the gate. But the gate was very difficult to open, for it had not been used since the green stone wall had been built around the village. Princess Shayna tried with all her strength to open the gate, but it would not budge. With help from the villagers, the gate opened slowly. It revealed a path that once had followed the serenely flowing stream, but now was overgrown and choked with weeds.

Princess Shayna could see that the path would be as difficult to travel as the other three paths. But she knew the effort would be worthwhile, for she always had her goal in sight. As the villagers watched Princess Shayna leave the shelter of their village, they rejoiced in her enthusiasm for her journey, for they had learned that was how she always approached life!

Feeling very good and confident about themselves, the villagers called to the Princess, "Wait, we want to help you!" And they began to systematically tear down their green stone wall. "We will use the stones to pave a new path to the Village of the Yellow Sunflowers. We no longer need a wall around our village to separate us from the other villages. We have learned to value our gifts because

len Birnbaum

of your Invisible Visible Gift and wish to share them with the other villages," the villagers exclaimed.

"Look up," Peridot said. The villagers stopped paving and curiously looked to the sky. "Our new path lights up the ominous cloud that has shadowed the brightness of the kingdom."

But only Peridot detected the mysterious raven concealing itself behind the ominous cloud. Peridot had also observed the bird secretly circling over the village every day since Princess Shayna had arrived. Every time Peridot saw the raven circling over the village, he felt a chill go through his entire body. He was curious but told no one, for he did not want to concern anyone else.

"I will guide you and the villagers toward the village of the Yellow Sunflowers," White Falcon told Princess Shayna as he excitedly jumped off her shoulder. He extended his powerful wings and glided gracefully above the princess and the villagers as they paved the new path.

Peridot told Princess Shayna, "The villagers are very proud of the bright new path they are building to connect the Village of the Green Healing Herbs to the Village of the Yellow Sunflowers."

You will find reflections about this chapter
on page 115 of the Gift Giver's Guide.

Journey Home

Princess Shayna and Peridot followed the green brick path to the Village of the Yellow Sunflowers. As they walked along the path, White Falcon told Princess Shayna, "I am so proud of you. The circle of your Vision Quest is complete. You visited all the villages and have met the royal advisors' challenge and achieved your goal of living and working with all the villagers. Your vision and goal have been successful."

"Thank you, White Falcon," Princess Shayna said gratefully. "You're so right. The villagers have accepted and shared my Invisible Visible Gift. They tore down their stone walls and built new paths to connect their villages. Now, I am confident that someday I will be able to guide and care for the Kingdom of Kindness with the cooperation and understanding of all four villages.

"I know the four village emissaries will use all their unique gifts to help us safely return to the royal castle by the second day of the second month of the new year," the princess said to White Falcon.

"Not much time remains! We must not get lost in the Forest of Fear again," Princess Shayna said as she felt a chilling shiver go through her entire body. "I will never forget the frightening experience I had when the evil woodsmen deceived me."

"Now, I am wiser and more aware because of our encounter with that devious duo. I will tell Citrine, Spinel, Padparadscha, and Peridot about the joys of the Forest of Friendship and the risks of the Forest of Fear. I will caution them to beware of the evil woodsmen. We must also remain alert at all times for their malicious mentor, Meevillain. The treacherous trio could appear anywhere and at anytime during the final days of my Vision Quest," Princess Shayna said.

For three days, Princess Shayna and White Falcon traveled to the other villages where the village emissaries eagerly waited to accompany them on their journey home.

When they finally returned to the Village of the Yellow Sunflowers, Princess Shayna and her companions were exhausted. Everyone was exhilarated about their journey together, which would begin early the next morning. They all had a good night's rest until, just before daybreak, Princess Shayna was suddenly awakened by a chilling wind whirling around her.

"Rimsiyavyo!" Princess Shayna exclaimed. "I know the answer! I have solved the problem! It was Meevillain who created the ominous dark cloud. It was her Cloud of Chaos that has shadowed the brightness of the entire Kingdom of Kindness since my birth!"

White Falcon, Citrine, Spinel, Padparadscha, and Peridot were awakened by Princess Shayna's exclamation. Princess Shayna told her companions her theory— from the moment Meevillain gave the nuptial nectar to her parents to that very moment of self-knowledge. They all listened carefully and now fully understood the source of mistrust and misunderstanding between the villages.

Then Citrine, Spinel, Padparadscha, and Peridot told the Princess that they too had noticed a change in Meevillain's Cloud of Chaos. "From the moment you arrived in our villages, the Cloud of Chaos has been evaporating and growing smaller every day. It must be because of the sharing of our gifts."

"That must be the answer. Throughout my Vision Quest, the kingdom has become brighter with the reflection of the villagers and the gifts we shared," Princess Shayna said.

Then Citrine said, "I often detected a mysterious raven darting behind the ominous Cloud of Chaos. I also saw the mysterious bird secretly circling over the village every day after you arrived in my village, Princess Shayna. Every time I saw the raven, I felt a chill go through my entire body. I was very worried, but I did not want to worry anyone else."

Then Spinel, Padparadscha, and Peridot made the identical revelations. "We all must be watchful and aware of that mysterious raven, for it is Meevillain!" they said to one another.

Princess Shayna warned them, "Now, you must remember everything I have told you. I know you are very eager and excited to help me get home, but it might be a perilous journey. You now know how malicious Meevillain is!"

Her companions said, "Princess Shayna, you told us the joys of the Forest of Friendship and risks of the Forest of Fear. We are willing and able to handle any obstacle we have to overcome to help you return home safely."

Then the four emissaries sang in unison:

*"We'll work with one another,
We will do our very best.
With all our special gifts,
You'll complete your Vision Quest!"*

Princess Shayna and her companions were almost ready to leave the Village of the Yellow Sunflowers where she had begun her journey almost an entire year before. Now the little amethyst-colored velvet bag Poppy had given her was almost empty, and her golden necklace was almost completely filled with pearls.

While Princess Shayna and her companions were preparing for their journey into the Forest of Friendship, they were entertained by White Falcon riding the powerful wind that seemed to be coming from somewhere deep within the Forest of Friendship. As they watched the magnificent bird soar on the powerful wind, they became more eager and determined about their journey.

Princess Shayna and her companions did not know that the powerful wind that White Falcon enjoyed soaring on was caused by Meevillain's whirling upset about her diminishing Cloud of Chaos. Meevillain ranted, "I am outraged by Princess Shayna's successful sharing of her Invisible Visible Gift with all the villages. I am infuriated that all four villages tore down their stone walls and built paths along the serenely flowing streams to connect the villages again. And I am furious that all the villagers warmly welcomed each village emissary into each other's villages, as they had in the past."

Meevillain was totally consumed by her scheme to stop the princess and her companions from reaching the royal castle. "I will have to use all my evil powers and secret magic spells to lure Princess Shayna and her companions into my Forest of Fear. I will trick them myself, without Mennis and Meene! I will make sure Princess Shayna never returns home from my Forest of Fear! This time I will not fail! This is my last chance to keep my Cloud of Chaos shadowing the Kingdom of Kindness and make the entire Kingdom of Kindness mine," Meevillain pledged.

The next morning, as the sun was rising with a new brightness, a familiar gentle breeze caressed Princess Shayna's face. She was awakened by White Falcon's powerful wings flapping up and down with excitement. As he perched on her shoulder, Princess Shayna gently stroked his majestic head and told her beloved and devoted companion, "I love you more than tongue can tell."

Then he soared into the sky, drawing Princess Shayna's attention to the brightening sunlight. This time Princess Shayna had seen the light of truth. Now, they both felt the warm glow of a sunrise coming from behind the slowly diminishing Cloud of Chaos that had shadowed the kingdom since the princess was born.

"Yes, my theory about Meevillain's Cloud of Chaos proved to be true! I cannot wait to get home and tell everyone what I have discovered," Princess Shayna said.

What Princess Shayna did not know was that Raven Meevillain had flown over the kingdom to spy on her and methodically memorize the progress of her Vision Quest. She was very agitated, anxious, and annoyed by the princess's success. Each day her anger and fear of failure made her more determined to stop the princess from returning home.

Meevillain was fiercely aware of the change in her Cloud of Chaos. "I feel as if my evil spirit, my sinister spells, and my Cloud of Chaos are all evaporating. I do not feel the potency I did when the princess began her Vision Quest," Meevillain said angrily. At times Meevillain would become so incensed that she would whirl herself into a frenzy.

Princess Shayna and her companions noticed the change in the wind, but they were so engrossed in their goal that they did not give the wind much consideration. They were feeling so good about themselves and each other that they ignored the disturbance and continued to share their gifts. This response totally exasperated and exhausted Meevillain, who thought her wicked wind would frighten them into abandoning Princess Shayna.

To the contrary, everyone was very excited to begin the homeward journey. It had been decided that each village emissary would contribute his or her unique gifts to help complete Princess Shayna's Vision Quest.

Princess Shayna asked, "Citrine, will you organize all the responsibilities for our return journey?"

"Yes, I will be proud to be accountable for all the details and organize a perfect plan," Citrine replied.

Then Citrine asked Spinel, "Will you make sure that all of us are comfortable and cared for? Our journey could be difficult, and we will need you to remind everyone what a good job we are doing and encourage us to remember our goal!"

Spinel was feeling so good about herself, she said, "Yes, I can help keep everyone from becoming anxious or uncomfortable with one another. I will help you keep the sense of friendship and harmony."

84

Then Citrine told Padparadscha, "You will be the perfect courageous pathfinder because there is a great risk of encountering the treacherous trio who live in the Forest of Fear. Will you help Sarah Spundah lead us on our journey through the Forest of Friendship?"

Padparadscha was feeling so good about himself that he said confidently, "I will gladly take directions from Sarah Spundah. Princess Shayna has told me how wise and skillful Sarah Spundah is."

Then Citrine told Peridot, "You have been keeping a daily journal of Princess Shayna's Vision Quest. It makes sense that you should continue your chronicle."

Peridot was feeling so good about himself that he said, "Yes, I shall continue writing my journal." Then Peridot thought to himself, "I am confident that Princess Shayna's Vision Quest will become a great heroic legend and will be read by people from many distant lands. It will be her legacy by which she will guide and care for the Kingdom of Kindness."

Now they were finally ready to leave the Village of the Yellow Sunflowers and begin the final portion of Princess Shayna's Vision Quest. They left the village with great enthusiasm, for Princess Shayna's approach to life was very contagious.

White Falcon flew ahead of the princess and her four companions. There was a spectacular radiance surrounding them as they walked the same path the princess had walked almost a year before.

As they walked along the path, Princess Shayna recalled the beginning of her Vision Quest and the time she had spent with all the villagers. Now she was becoming very excited to see Sarah Spundah and her forest friends who had saved her from Meevillain's mysterious sleeping mist and the woodmen's treacherous trickery!

As the village emissaries and the princess joyfully walked along the path together, the white falcon soared higher and higher on the powerful wind. The air currents seemed to grow stronger and stronger as they got closer to the Forest of Friendship.

As they neared the Forest of Friendship, Princess Shayna realized what had caused such wind-swept conditions. "Rimsiyavyo! It is Meevillain's anxiousness about our arrival. She must be very angry about her Cloud of Chaos evaporating," Princess Shayna warned.

The stronger the winds, the higher the white falcon soared! He was such a beautiful and majestic sight. The vision of his strong white wings lifting him to higher altitudes strengthened everyone's attitudes about their journey.

Suddenly, they realized that they could see how high White Falcon was flying. "Look, Meevillain's Cloud of Chaos is evaporating before our eyes," Padparadscha said. "The stronger we feel about ourselves, the higher White Falcon flies."

Princess Shayna exclaimed, "Look at yourselves! The smaller the Cloud of Chaos, the brighter the illumination around you."

The village emissaries looked at each other and saw themselves in a radiant light they had never seen before! They were empowered and enlightened by a sense of peacefulness and wisdom about themselves and their purpose as never before.

You will find reflections about this chapter
on page 116 of the Gift Giver's Guide.

The Path

Suddenly, there was another radiant reflection before them. It was Sarah Spundah's little silver form sleeping in the middle of a splendid silken silver spider web that marked the entrance into the Forest of Friendship. When White Falcon saw her reflection, he gracefully soared down toward the entrance to the Forest of Friendship.

White Falcon was so happy to see Sarah Spundah that he extended his huge white wings and began to flap them with excitement. The gentle breeze from the movement of his powerful wings and Princess Shayna's sweet whispers of friendship awakened Sarah Spundah to the joyful sight of her beloved friends and their companions.

Sarah Spundah stretched her fragile, ancient arachnid legs and slowly opened her splendid silver lace web into the Forest of Friendship for Princess Shayna and her companions. "All your forest friends will be delighted see you," Sarah Spundah said sweetly. "They have been busily gathering all kinds of nuts, berries, and fruit for a celebration feast in honor of your long awaited return."

Princess Shayna gently put Sarah Spundah in the pocket close to her heart and said, "Please guide us through the forest just as you did before."

With Sarah's help, Princess Shayna, White Falcon, Citrine, Spinel, Padparadscha, and Peridot moved quickly through the Forest of Friendship to avoid Meevillain. Princess Shayna suddenly stopped to listen. "Sarah, listen. I thought I heard a conversation. It's not the sound the forest creatures make. It sounded like two men talking," the princess said.

"Do not be concerned, Princess Shayna," Sarah Spundah replied. "You no longer have to worry about Meevillain's two evil woodsmen, whom she called Mennis and Meene. She was so angry about their failure and your escape from her Forest of Fear that she turned those greedy, treacherous trolls into worms. Meevillain then commanded Mennis and Meene to crawl back into the slime underneath the large moss-covered rock where they had lived before she had transformed them into woodsmen."

"Oh, I am so relieved that we will not have to worry about Mennis and Meene," Princess Shayna said. "But we must continue on and find out where the conversation is coming from."

Low and behold, when they got to the center of the forest, there were all the villagers from the four different villages. "Rimsiyavyo!" Princess Shayna said. "How did you all get here?"

The villagers explained, "We were so grateful for your Invisible Visible Gift that we decided to take the stones that remained after we paved our new paths to the other villages and use them to build a multicolored path through the Forest of Friendship. Now we will pave a multicolored stone path back to the royal castle for you."

"We will work together to help you complete your Vision Quest and arrive home safely. Our single path will become a permanent multicolored symbol of our agreement to respect and value ourselves and each other," the village elders said. Princess Shayna was speechless. She was overwhelmed by the villagers cooperation and commitment to her and to themselves.

Everyone enjoyed a Forest of Friendship celebration. The villagers danced with joy and sang songs about the transformations in their lives. They proudly told Sarah Spundah and her forest friends all about their accomplishments. Princess Shayna told the entire story of Meevillain's Cloud of Chaos to Sarah Spundah and her forest friends. Then she asked, "Sarah Spundah, have you noticed a change in Meevillain's Cloud of Chaos that has shadowed the kingdom since my birth?"

Sarah said, "Yes, I have noticed the change in Meevillain's Cloud of Chaos. Surprisingly, there also has been another change in the Forest of Friendship. Vegetation has begun to grow and bloom again everywhere Meevillain had created her Forest of Fear!" To Princess Shayna, she said, "The word throughout the forest is that Meevillain has remained in her raven form since the very day White Falcon and I rescued you from her Forest of Fear. Every day since then, Meevillain has left the Forest of Fear and circled over the village where you were living."

"We discovered that also," Princess Shayna said.

"But there is more you do not know," Sarah continued. "Whenever Meevillain returned to the Forest of Fear, each tree or bush where she had perched the night before had begun to grow again from the brightness that had filtered throughout the canopy of the Forest of Friendship. It seemed as if there were no room for Meevillain and her fear in the Forest of Friendship!"

Princess Shayna said, "Although Mennis and Meene are no longer a threat to completing my Vision Quest, I must still beware of Meevillain. I know too well that she can still create her Forest of Fear at any time, in any part of the Forest of Friendship."

Sarah said, "I will continue to accompany all of you through the Forest of Friendship."

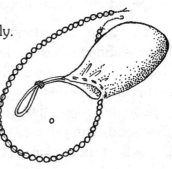

Princess Shayna replied, "We need to travel very quickly. Two nights before, as I reached into my amethyst-colored velvet bag, I discovered that I only had three pearls left. Tonight there will be only one ! We must return to the royal castle by tomorrow, for it will be the second day of the second month of the new year. I must keep my agreement," Princess Shayna said.

Then all the villagers sang to Princess Shayna in unison,

"We'll work with one another,
We will do our very best.
With all our special gifts,
You'll complete your Vision Quest!"

The villagers worked very hard. And the closer the princess got to the royal castle, the faster Meevillian whirled her wicked wind, but to no avail. The princess and her companions would not be detained. They continued to cooperatively and confidently pave their multicolored path through the Forest of Friendship. By the end of the day, they were all exhausted.

All day long the villagers had tried not to be concerned and distracted by the wicked wind of Meevillain's discontent. They did notice that the wicked wind was accompanied by an unusually warm glow of sunlight that filtered through the forest's lush green canopy. The warmth of the sunlight brightened everyone's spirits and calmed their uneasiness.

"Princess Shayna, you and the villagers must settle down on the moss beds the forest creatures have prepared for you. You will need all your strength tomorrow!" Sarah advised gently.

"Sarah, we know how wise you are, and we will rest so we can complete my Vision Quest tomorrow," Princess Shayna said respectfully.

Just before Princess Shayna and her companions went to sleep in their comfortable campsite, Citrine reminded the emissaries of their responsibilities. Spinel encouraged them with inspiring praise of their accomplishments and abilities. Peridot said he would be up early to write in his journal about Princess Shayna's courageous journey, and Padparadscha exclaimed that he would be ready to find the perfect path back to the royal castle with Sarah Spundah.

Princess Shayna told the villagers, "I am very proud of you and how you have continued to share your unique gifts and my Invisible Visible Gift with one another. I am confident that you will help me to return home on time."

Sarah Spundah said, "I, too, will be rested and ready to spin my way with Padparadscha and help you return home on time."

Everyone was getting ready to go to sleep when White Falcon jumped off Princess Shayna's shoulder and flapped his wings with excitement. With his powerful wings, he rose above all the inhabitants of the forest. He knew he must remain alert and protect the princess on the last portion of her Vision Quest. Princess Shayna joyfully recognized this special signal that she had shared with White Falcon since her childhood. The princess knew she must rest before taking the last remaining steps on the radiant multicolored path that would lead her home. She fell asleep thinking about her homecoming.

In the darkness of the night, Raven Meevillain had perched high above the celebration and listened to Princess Shayna tell Sarah Spundah that there was only *one* pearl left. "And I have only *one* day left to stop Princess Shayna from returning home," Meevillain said to herself.

Meevillain had been watching Princess Shayna's every move. Each day her Cloud of Chaos grew smaller and her feelings of anxiousness and agitation grew larger. Meevillain said to herself, "Every night when I return to my Forest of Fear, many of the trees and bushes are no longer twisted and bare, and new leaves have sprouted on their straight strong branches. Even the paths that once went in circles and or led to dead ends have begun to connect to one another along the stream that once again serenely flows through the Forest of Friendship. I am exhausted from my attempts to frighten and mislead the Princess and her companions, and I am upset by the unexplainable condition of my Forest of Fear. Before daybreak I will create a terrible uneasiness and disturbance throughout the entire Forest of Friendship! This is my last chance to confront Princess Shayna. I will stop her from returning home," Meevillain vowed in a terrible rage.

Then she flew off to rest on the last remaining branch of her favorite twisted elder tree. "I must gather all my strength and evil spirits to whirl the most furious wicked wind I have ever created. But first, I must cast another mysterious sleeping mist over the entire Forest of Friendship and all its inhabitants, including *that meddling* white falcon. This time, even he will not be able to protect his beloved princess," Meevillain cackled.

Meevillain's wicked wind dispensed her mysterious sleeping mist over the entire forest, and all the inhabitants fell into a dangerously deep sleep.

Princess Shayna awoke just before daybreak, excited about her homecoming. "I think I will take a walk and not awaken my companions. They have worked so hard to help me on my journey home," Princess Shayna said to herself.

Suddenly the earth shook and the trees bent with the unrivaled force of Meevillain's last attempt to challenge Princess Shayna. The princess circled her hands over her silver candles three times to illuminate her path. She was so engrossed in finding out where the mysterious disturbance was coming from that she did not notice that no one, including White Falcon, had awakened.

As the princess walked away from the campsite, Meevillain changed herself back into her human form and appeared in front of the large moss-covered rock, blocking Princess Shayna's path. She was dressed in her raven-colored velvet cloak and carried her triple-twisted wooden staff. She was quite a frightening sight to behold.

At first, Princess Shayna was shocked at such a dreadful sight. She said to herself, "Here I am all *alone* with Meevillain! I must remember my parents' loving words and their encouragement to face my fears for now I must face my greatest fear!" Princess Shayna and her companions had not seen Meevillain throughout their entire return journey through the Forest of Friendship. The villagers had hoped that Meevillain would not appear at all. But deep in her heart, Princess Shayna knew that this moment would come, that she would have to face Meevillain before she could return home and complete her Vision Quest.

"Why are you not sleeping?" Meevillain demanded. "I have spread my most powerful mysterious sleeping mist over the entire Forest of Friendship!"

"Meevillain, your evil magic has lost its power. All the villagers have learned to share my Invisible Visible Gift," Princess Shayna replied proudly.

Even though she knew the answer, Princess Shayna courageously said, "Meevillain, I know that you transformed yourself into your raven form and followed me on my Vision Quest after your sinister scheme with Mennis and Meene failed. What is it that you want now?"

Meevillain scowled, "I want the power you will have if you complete your Vision Quest and prove yourself worthy to become queen. Ever since your father married your mother all my plans have been spoiled! If I keep you from completing your journey, your parents will be overwhelmed with grief, and unable to guide and care for the kingdom. Sigmund will die of a broken heart. Then I will become the royal wizard and rule the kingdom. Then I will finally have what I have always wanted. And I will feel good about myself!"

At that very moment, the sun began to rise over the Kingdom of Kindness. The light was even brighter than ever before. Even through the heavy mysterious sleeping mist, Princess Shayna could hear the wind in the trees singing a song of gladness and see the newly straightened branches of the trees and bushes dancing with their beautiful new-sprung leaves. Then some twigs began to fall to the ground and gently awaken Princess Shayna's sleeping companions.

"My mysterious sleeping mist is evaporating and my evil spell is broken," Meevillain cried in bewilderment.

White Falcon, Sarah Spundah, and all the villagers were awakened by the sunlight illuminating their faces. The brightness of their Invisible Visible Gifts reflected onto Meevillain. Even her raven-colored hood could not protect her.

Meevillain was blinded by their radiance and flew into a wild rage that sent her whirling into the air forming a fearsome raven-colored funnel. Her raven-colored cloaked figure whirled faster and faster breaking through the forest's lush green canopy and into the bright azure sky. She whirled directly through the remaining mysterious sleeping mist and into the last remnant of her Cloud of Chaos.

"I must protect Princess Shayna before Meevillain tries to harm her," White Falcon said to himself. And he ascended into the last remnant of the Cloud of Chaos.

Princess Shayna saw White Falcon take flight, then disappear through the mysterious sleeping mist into the Cloud of Chaos! Suddenly there was a flash of lightening and a loud explosion of thunder. Meevillain and White Falcon continued to tumble uncontrollably through the turbulence.

"I can see White Falcon pursuing Meevillain into the turbulent Cloud of Chaos," said Sarah Spundah.

As everyone tried to follow the white falcon's flight, the princess began to weep tears of sadness. "I can no longer see White Falcon. He has disappeared into Meevillain's turbulent Cloud of Chaos," she cried. "Now I will have to face my deepest fear—life without my beloved and devoted companion would be more than I could bare!" Tremendous tears of sadness rolled down her fairy-kissed cheeks.

Then, for the first time since Princess Shayna was born, the sun's welcoming warm rays filtered down through the entire Forest of Friendship. All the villagers and forest creatures were astonished by the brightness. As they looked upward, the brilliant warmth that radiated from their faces and their multicolored path immediately reflected upward into the sky, creating a magnificent rainbow of orange, yellow, blue, and green. It was the first rainbow anyone had ever seen.

Suddenly, Princess Shayna felt a familiar gentle breeze caress her face. It was White Falcon flapping his wings with excitement as he circled Princess Shayna and the villagers. The magnificent bird was a splendid sight to behold as he soared through the brilliant multicolored rainbow!

Princess Shayna reached out to her companion who had courageously risked his life to save hers. She felt a love and gratitude toward him that she had never known before. White Falcon came to rest on Princess Shayna's shoulder. As she gently stroked his majestic head, she said, "How grateful we are that you met the greatest challenge of my Vision Quest and saved my life, again."

Then White Falcon whispered to Princess Shayna, "I risked my life because I love you more than tongue can tell."

Realizing that Meevillain and her Cloud of Chaos had evaporated, everyone rejoiced with great relief that she would no longer threaten the completion of Princess Shayna's Vision Quest. Sarah Spundah and all the forest creatures joined the villagers in a song of joy and thanksgiving.

"The sun is shining,
The sun is shining,
White Falcon, saved the day!
Meevillain and her cloud are gone,
Hooray, Hooray, Hooray!"

Everyone was jubilant and rejoiced with great enthusiasm!

Sarah Spundah said, "My forest friends will gather fruits, berries, and nuts for a delicious breakfast celebration!"

"Princess Shayna, I know you are very excited. Please, do no forget to dispense your silver apricot potion," Sarah Spundah said sweetly.

"Thank you, Sarah Spundah. In the excitement, I almost forgot," Princess Shayna said gratefully.

After everyone had finished eating, they happily prepared for the last portion of Princess Shayna's Vision Quest and her return home. Citrine organized everyone, Spinel inspired them with words of praise, Peridot quickly recorded the extraordinary events of the morning, and Padparadscha accompanied Sarah Spundah ahead of the others to find the shortest and easiest path back home to the royal castle!

The sun's welcoming warm rays, the reflection of the villagers, their multicolored path, and the brilliant rainbow embraced The Forest of Friendship. Soon Princess Shayna, White Falcon and Sarah Spundah were following the villagers' multicolored path that did not twist or turn into dead ends or go in circles like the paths in Meevillain's Forest of Fear, but was straight and true.

You will find reflections about this chapter
on page 117 of the Gift Giver's Guide.

Celebration

"Our daughter is almost home," King Alexander and Queen Sylvia exclaimed joyfully when they saw the rainbow shining above their entire Kingdom of Kindness. While everyone in the royal castle had been preparing for Princess Shayna's return, they had been watching Meevillain's Cloud of Chaos diminish!

With White Falcon safely perched on her shoulder, Princess Shayna, Citrine, Spinel and Peridot quickly followed Sarah Spundah and Padparadscha along the multicolored path that lead them out of the Forest of Friendship. Princess Shayna became very excited when they reached the edge of the Forest of Friendship and she saw the royal castle through Sarah Spundah's silver spider web.

"Look, I can see the copper roof tops of the royal castle glistening in the bright sunlight. Yellow, orange, blue, and green banners are flying from the tower turrets. What a glorious homecoming," she exclaimed.

The princess ran down the same path she had walked a year ago as she began her Vision Quest. As she got closer to the royal castle, the large green courtyard gate swung open. There stood her parents, whom she had not seen for an entire year. Their faces were beaming with love and pride, and their arms were opened wide to welcome their daughter home.

"I feel like my heart will leap out of my body," she said to White Falcon.

White Falcon showed his excitement by jumping off Princess Shayna's shoulder and soaring over the tower turrets bedecked with the colorful banners. "What a beautiful sight to behold. The Kingdom has not known such happiness since Princess Shayna's birth," White Falcon said to himself.

The princess rushed into her parents' outstretched arms. Tears of joy ran down Queen Sylvia's face as she and King Alexander hugged their daughter close to their hearts. Princess Shayna looked up at her father, took his face in her hands and gave him their traditional kisses on both cheeks. Queen Sylvia lovingly gazed at her

daughter to see how she had grown in a year. The queen was so grateful that her daughter had returned home safely.

"I feel so wonderfully safe and secure inside these peaceful ivy-covered walls," Princess Shayna said.

Mimi, Poppy, Sigmund the Royal Wizard, and Mac stood alongside her parents. Their faces lit up with delight as they hugged the princess close to their hearts.

Then Sarah and all the villagers quickly followed behind the princess and were greeted warmly by King Alexander and Queen Sylvia. Padparadscha carried Sarah Spundah on his shoulder, for the ancient arachnid was very tired from the morning's excitement.

Sarah sweetly told the King and Queen, "I am delighted to see you all so happy again. Yes, just like the lily of the valley that grows in the Garden of Knowledge, happiness has returned to the Kingdom of Kindness."

As Princess Shayna entered the castle courtyard and walked through the Garden of Knowledge, the sun sparkled brightly over the Kingdom of Kindness. The rainbow remained as a brilliant banner in the cloudless azure sky to symbolize the villagers' cooperation and Princess Shayna's successful completion of her Vision Quest.

Princess Shayna gazed upon the rainbow and smiled as she gently ran her fingers over her pearl necklace. "My completed add-a-pearl necklace will always be a symbol of my Vision Quest on which I learned a deeper sense of patience and wisdom," she told White Falcon. "I feel a greater understanding and awareness about myself, my family and my life. These little pearls will always remind me of my mother's tears of joy when I returned home, and my tears of joy when I knew you were not lost forever in Meevillain's Cloud of Chaos."

When her parents joined her in the garden, she asked them, "How did you know I would complete my Vision Quest successfully?"

King Alexander and Queen Sylvia told her, "We had great confidence in your ability to achieve your goal because of your Invisible Visible Gift. We knew you would complete your Vision Quest and demonstrate to the royal advisors that you were caring and competent enough to someday be queen of the Kingdom of Kindness."

"Thank you for your trust, your love, and my Invisible Visible Gift," Princess Shayna told her parents.

One by one, the royal advisors proceeded to the garden through the joyful crowd of villagers who were singing and dancing in celebration of Princess Shayna's success. As they greeted the royal family each royal advisor said, "Congratulations, Princess Shayna! You kept your agreement and arrived home on the second day of the second month of the new year. Now you must tell us about your Vision Quest!"

Princess Shayna began, "We no longer need to wonder or worry about the ominous cloud that shadowed our kingdom. It will never appear again! Meevillain created that shadow with her ominous Cloud of Chaos, but she evaporated into her own evil spell! The last remnants of her wretchedness produced the rainbow that now embraces the entire kingdom. Meevillain's life of solitude, sorrow, and sorcery caused all the melancholy, misunderstanding, and mistrust in our kingdom. As the villagers began to share my Invisible Visible Gifts and value their own gifts, Meevillain's evil powers began to evaporate just like her Cloud of Chaos. White Falcon's bravery and the villagers courage broke Meevillain's evil spell that eventually would have destroyed our kingdom. I am so grateful to White Falcon, all the villagers, Sarah Spundah, and her forest friends for saving my life and helping me complete my Vision Quest and return happiness to the Kingdom of Kindness.

"I know you have many questions about my Vision Quest," she said to the royal advisors. "As you instructed, I brought the four village emissaries and their gifts home with me. I am confident that the village emissaries will brilliantly answer all your questions and share their most praiseworthy gifts with you. Because they represent each of our villages, you know that they are as valuable and exceptional as the sapphire gemstones for which they are named. At each village farewell celebration, I was presented with a magnificent, brightly colored key that represents the key to the villagers' hearts and their homes. It was a token of their appreciation for my understanding and respecting their perspectives and lifestyle, a generous gift to show their acceptance of me into their community, and a gift of gratefulness for sharing my Invisible Visible Gift that enhanced all the villagers' self-esteem," Princess Shayna said.

"Princess Shayna has recognized and understood the uniqueness of each of our villages," Citrine said proudly. "We have many extraordinary stories of how she graciously and unselfishly used her Invisible Visible Gift to help the villagers recognize their own gifts."

"We have the deepest admiration for Princess Shayna and White Falcon," Spinel said. "The greatest testimonial of Princess Shayna's ability to become queen is her total acceptance of each villager with whom she shared her Invisible Visible Gift. She accepted us for who we are and what we value. The princess helped everyone in the Kingdom of Kindness feel good about themselves and build their self-esteem."

"Jani the Queen of the Flower Fairies was right. The Invisible Visible Gift is a beautiful, but fragile circle of life. It is more valuable than any gift we could receive, a gift that could not be bought, sold, or even taken away by Meevillain, Mennis, or Meene," Padparadscha added.

"Princess Shayna shared her Invisible Visible Gift with all the villagers because she knew we were willing to accept such a unique gift. One by one, as we shared it with each other, the princess's Invisible Visible Gift became visible upon each one of us," Peridot said proudly.

Citrine, Spinel, Peridot, and Padparadscha told King Alexander and Queen Sylvia, "Princess Shayna truly is a gift to the entire kingdom. We will always be thankful to you and the royal advisors for listening to the princess and sending her on her Vision Quest."

Then all the villagers cheered in agreement, "Hooray for Princess Shayna, our future queen!"

"King Alexander and Queen Sylvia, your daughter lived and worked with all the villagers and gave them more than they dreamed possible. Princess Shayna has proven that some day she will be a perfect queen to guide and care for the Kingdom of Kindness!" the four royal advisors proclaimed.

Humbly, Peridot reached into his large green sack and took out his journal. He said respectfully, "King Alexander and Queen Sylvia, this is my gift to the Kingdom of Kindness. It is a perfectly written account of Princess Shayna's Vision Quest. Because Princess Shayna shared her Invisible Visible Gift with me and my village, I feel good enough about myself and my most praiseworthy gifts that I wish to honor your daughter by sharing my journal with you. I have called my story, *Princess Shayna's Invisible Visible Gift,* and I give it to you for safekeeping.

"*Princess Shayna's Invisible Visible Gift,* what a wonderful gift, Peridot!" said the queen.

"Thank you, Peridot. We are confident that your journal will become very meaningful for the people from distant lands to learn from. Most importantly, it will become a great heroic legend by which Princess Shayna will some day guide and care for all the people of the kingdom," King Alexander said.

"King Alexander, I have learned that all the villages honor and respect the wisdom of their elders. It is from the wisdom of their stories that we learn the most about ourselves and our traditions. Do you think it would be appropriate for the village elders to teach and share Princess Shayna's heroic legend with all the children in the kingdom?" Citrine asked proudly.

"Yes, indeed, Citrine. Thank you for your splendid idea!" said the king.

"Every year, on the second day of the second month of the new year *Princess Shayna's Invisible Visible Gift* will be told throughout the kingdom by the village elders," King Alexander proclaimed.

"To commemorate the story of *Princess Shayna's Invisible Visible Gift,* could all the villages of the kingdom join together and celebrate with a grand festival?" Spinel asked thoughtfully.

"Yes, indeed, Spinel. Thank you for your lovely idea!" Queen Sylvia said. "The story will be told as a remembrance of this joyous occasion!"

"I think a festival sounds so exciting! Do you think all the villagers could dress up in multicolored costumes?" Padparadscha asked enthusiastically. "It would be great fun for the children to perform the story and whenever the village elder says 'Meevillain,' everyone can shake noisemakers or stamp their feet to show their displeasure. I know everyone would have such a good time!"

"Yes, indeed, Padparadscha. Thank you for your very clever ideas!" said the king. "Laughter and enjoyment are significant in our lives, but we must never forget the lessons we all have learned because of Meevillain and her ominous Cloud of Chaos."

"I will prepare special celebration pastries—heart-shaped poppy seed cookies," Mimi added. "They will be a symbol of the many seeds of sharing that Princess Shayna planted so the villagers' hearts could blossom with understanding and respect for themselves and one another."

"I am so honored by your thoughtfulness and so delighted that *every year* there will be festivities to celebrate my Vision Quest. It makes my heart sing to know that the village elders will always tell my story to the young people. I want them to know how the villagers courageously overcame great obstacles and turned them into opportunities to value themselves, each other, and their most praiseworthy gifts," Princess Shayna said graciously.

All the villagers cheered in agreement, "Hooray for King Alexander and Queen Sylvia!"

"We trust that Princess Shayna will continue to share her Invisible Visible Gift with the villagers of the kingdom and the many visitors from distant lands," Queen Sylvia said.

"And we know she and White Falcon will have many more exciting journeys ahead of them before Princess Shayna becomes queen of the Kingdom of Kindness," King Alexander added.

Peridot quietly observed everyone celebrating with great jubilation and thought to himself, "Yes, it will be many years before Princess Shayna will guide and care for the people of the Kingdom of Kindness!

"Rimsiyavyo, that will be another story!"

You will find reflections about this chapter
on page 118 of the Gift Giver's Guide.

Gift Giver's Guide

Len Birnbaum

Village of the Orange Tiger Lilies

The villagers were feeling so good and confident about themselves that they called to the princess, "Wait, we all want to help you!" Then they began to eagerly tear down their orange stone wall.

"We will use the stones to pave a new path to the Village of the Green Healing Herbs. We no longer need a wall to separate us from the other villages. We have learned to value our gifts because of your Invisible Visible Gift, and we wish to share them with the other villages," the villagers exclaimed.

1. Why would you be comfortable or uncomfortable living in the Village of the Orange Tiger Lilies?

2. Do you know people who are similar to Padparadcha? Who are they?

Please unscramble **ASUCOGUROE** to enthusiastically understand the villagers in the story and the people in your life.

(courageous)

114

Village of the Green Healing Herbs

"I am impressed with the competency of the village. Look at the homes and shops. They all have architecturally correct green window flower boxes, diverse shades of green weather shutters, and geometrically shaped green door bells. All the buildings are built to increase efficiency and respect everyone's privacy," Princess Shayna told White Falcon.

1. Why would you be comfortable or uncomfortable living in the Village of the Green Healing Herbs?

2. Do you know people who are similar to Peridot? Who are they?

Please unscramble **CALIGOL** to accurately understand the villagers in the story and the people in your life.

(logical)

Journey Home

The village emissaries were empowered and enlightened by a sense of peacefulness and wisdom about themselves and their purpose, as never before.

1. Which village emissary would you like to be?

2. What are your most praiseworthy gifts?

Please unscramble **OCPREONTAIO** and reflect how it is relevant in the story and why it helps to build self-esteem in your life.

(cooperation)

The Path

White Falcon was a splendid sight to behold as he soared through the brilliant multicolored rainbow!

1. How did you feel in the Forest of Friendship during Princess Shayna's journey home?

2. Why did you feel that way?

Please unscramble **INUTSHEMSA** and reflect how it is contagious in the story and why it helps to build self-esteem in your life.

(enthusiasm)

Celebration

"Thank you for your trust, your love, and my Invisible Visible Gift," Princess Shayna told her parents.

1. What are some of the lessons you have learned from sharing Princess Shayna's Vision Quest?

Please unscramble this word **LBEREACONIT** and reflect how it is meaningful in the story, why it helps to build self-esteem in your life, why it belongs in each of our lives!

(celebration)

118